W9-ACK-281

PRISON BOY

PRISON BOY

BOY

SHARON E. MᴄKAY

 annick press
toronto + new york + vancouver

We acknowledge the support of the Canada Council for the Arts, the Ontario Arts Council, and the Government of Canada through the Canada Book Fund (CBF) for our publishing activities.

ONTARIO ARTS COUNCIL
CONSEIL DES ARTS DE L'ONTARIO
an Ontario government agency
un organisme du gouvernement de l'Ontario

Cataloging in Publication

McKay, Sharon E., author
    Prison boy / Sharon E. McKay.

Issued in print and electronic formats.
ISBN 978-1-55451-731-2 (bound).–ISBN 978-1-55451-730-5 (pbk.).–
ISBN 978-1-55451-733-6 (pdf).–ISBN 978-1-55451-732-9 (html)

    I. Title.

PS8575.K2898P75 2015   jC813'.54   C2014-907155-8
                                                 C2014-907156-6

Distributed in Canada by: Published in the U.S.A. by:
Firefly Books Ltd.   Annick Press (U.S.) Ltd.
50 Staples Avenue, Unit 1   Distributed in the U.S.A. by:
Richmond Hill, ON   Firefly Books (U.S.) Inc.
L4B 1H1   P.O. Box 1338, Ellicott Station
                                 Buffalo, NY 14205

Printed in Canada

Visit us at: www.annickpress.com
Visit Sharon E. McKay at: www.sharonmckay.ca

Also available in e-book format. Please visit www.annickpress.com/ebooks.html
for more details. Or scan

MIX
Paper from
responsible sources
FSC® C004071
www.fsc.org

For Saeideh Ciabi,
a woman of great strength and courage.

*"The only thing necessary for the triumph
of evil is for good men to do nothing."*

Edmund Burke

Chapter 1

Two visitors arrived on the same day. Each, in her own way, would change the future of the Pink House.

The first was a prune-faced representative of the King. She stood on the porch of the orphanage flanked by two soldiers wearing empty faces. In a low, flat voice she demanded to speak to Bell. Seven-year-old Pax stood behind Bell's empty rocking chair and watched.

Tiny Mega, who was all of eight but no bigger than a five-year-old, bashed back the plastic sheets that made do as a door, and ran into the house. She raced across the great room, leapt over the sleeping mats, and stood in the doorway of Bell's office. "Bell, a lady wants to speak to you." Mega's voice wobbled. To her, soldiers were big and scary.

"Now what?" Bell grumbled. Her real name was Isabelle, but everyone, even the children, called her Bell. She had come from England many years ago. She ran the orphanage, which was not really an orphanage, at least not the kind of place where children hung out the windows crying to be fed. "It is our home. We are a family," she repeated. The government called it an orphanage and Bell, tired of the politics, shrugged. Really, what did it matter as long as they were left alone?

It was called the Pink House because it was, inside and out, pink. A long time ago someone had given Bell cans of pink paint. There were still some stored in the outhouse.

Santoso came up behind her. "Mega, what does that lady want?" Mango squished out of his cheeks and coated his lips.

"Come, come," urged Mega.

One by one, the children followed Mega and Santoso out onto the porch. They stood silently, looking at the woman and the soldiers.

At last Bell pushed aside the sheets of plastic and stood on the porch. The children moved closer to her, like little chicks gathering around a mother hen. Only Pax remained where he was, distant but watching.

"Can I help you?" Speaking in her most proper British voice, Bell put her hands on her hips and glared up at the woman. (Really, Bell had neither hips nor waist. Bell was short and round, like a puddle.)

"I am from Children's Services. Our great King has decided that people like you should go back to your own country." The woman's words were razor-sharp. Bell glared. "And what exactly do you mean by 'people like me'?" Her singsong voice was now a low growl.

"You Europeans, you think you know it all. Go back to where you came from and take care of your own orphans."

Pax braced himself for Bell's wrath to descend on the woman like a thunderstorm. He waited. He waited some more. He tipped his head just enough to peek out of the corner of his eyes. Bell's face was white with fury, but she said nothing. Pak's mouth fell open with astonishment.

The woman looked down at her clipboard and began to read questions from the top of the page.

"How many children are currently living here?"

"Six," growled Bell. She sounded like a dog before it bites.

"What are their names?" the woman asked without looking up.

Bell motioned to each child. "This is Mega, our only girl. Santoso, Guntur—they are twins. This is Bambang and . . ." She paused, her hand above a small boy.

"Bhima," said Pax. Bell was always forgetting about Bhima. Bell forgot lots of things.

"Yes, Bhima. And this is Pax, my best boy."

"Pax?" The woman raised a thin eyebrow.

"Paxton, after my father," said Bell, but not with the usual pride in her voice. That was odd.

"Yes, fine." The woman recorded each child's name.

The children stood in gloomy silence.

When she was finished, the woman said, "You may continue to operate, but you must not take in any more children."

"Really? How very kind. But perhaps the obvious has eluded you. We operate as an orphanage. What are we supposed to take in—orangutans?" Bell snorted.

"No, no, no," Pax whispered as he dropped his head.

The woman twitched her nose like a rat, then handed Bell a piece of paper. She left, and the two soldiers followed in her wake.

Bell scanned the paper, crumpled it into a ball, and pitched it in the ditch that ran alongside the orphanage. The children gathered around her.

"Will we be taken away?" Mega whispered. Her lips trembled.

"Not while I live and breathe." Bell gave the plastic door a good bash and left them standing on the porch.

The second visitor arrived at the Pink House a few hours later.

"Bell, Bell!" Mega ran back into Bell's office.

In a moment they were once again standing on the porch, Mega, Santoso, Guntur, Bambang, Bhima, and Pax. This time they were not afraid, only curious.

The old woman held up an infant boy. It lay naked on a rag. "Take it," she said. She had no teeth. She had a hump on her back, sunken cheeks, and foggy eyes.

Pax stood behind Bell and held his breath.

Bell looked down at the baby. It was stringy—all head and thin, jerky limbs. "It needs its mother's milk," she said.

"The mother is dead. You give me money." The woman thrust the baby at Bell.

Bell took a step back and narrowed her eyes. "I don't buy babies."

"Take it or I will drown it," she cackled.

Pax sucked in his breath. She did not hold the baby

properly. Its head dangled. Pax reached out, scooped the baby in his arms, and hugged it against his chest. The woman let out a howl.

"Pax, wait," said Bell.

"I want money!" the woman screeched.

"Go away before I call the police," Bell yelled right back.

Pax took the baby into the great room and sat on his mat. He rocked him in his arms. The baby made twittering sounds like a little bird. "Ca, ca, ca." He looked up at Pax with clear, big, brown eyes streaked with gold—like a baby lion's eyes.

"What can you see?" Pax whispered. Little bubbles appeared on the baby's lips. He smiled. Pax smiled back.

Bell stood above Pax. "It will likely die," she said, but gently.

"No he won't," said Pax.

"I don't want you to get hurt."

Pax looked up at Bell. "I don't feel hungry now," he said.

"Hungry? What are you talking about?"

"Being alone is like being hungry," he whispered.

Bell sighed. "Pax, I haven't the faintest idea what you are talking about. You are surrounded by people. We have enough food."

"I know, but holding him makes me . . ." He didn't know what to say. He didn't understand it himself. "He makes me feel—full." Pax rocked the baby back and forth.

"Oh for heaven's sake, you are talking in riddles. Mega, boil water and sterilize those old baby bottles in the cupboard. Let the water cool in the small tub and then bathe the baby. Check the temperature. No need to cook it," said Bell.

Mega nodded. She was young, but she could do things like use a sharp knife, boil water, and bathe babies.

"No, I will take care of him," said Pax.

Bell wasn't listening. She stormed off in search of her purse.

The other children looked at the infant over Pax's shoulder. Bambang, who was round with big cheeks (although he ate no more than the others), got down on his knees and touched the baby's face. "He's soft," he whispered.

"Pax, he looks like you. He has eyes like you. See the little yellow bits?" said Santoso.

"Maybe he's your true, true brother," added Guntur.

"That's right. And that woman was a fairy godmother," said Santoso.

Bambang shook his head. "She's not a fairy godmother. She's ugly and has no teeth."

Bell returned with a purse hooked over her arm and a kerchief on her head knotted under her chin. "I will go to the medical unit in the city and get some formula, but Pax, remember what I said. It will likely die."

"His name is Kai."

"Why Kai?" said Bell.

"He told me," replied Pax.

Bell sighed and shook her head. "Just remember what I said."

That is how Kai came to stay. From that moment on, Pax became Kai's guardian, his protector, his father, mother, and maybe his brother, too. Stranger things have happened.

As for Bell, it wasn't the first time she had deliberately ignored the government's regulations.

Chapter 2

Three years later

It was still dark. The sun funneled through a pinhole on the horizon.

Pax sat cross-legged on the porch listening to morning sounds—dogs barking, birds chirping, street sellers setting up shop. Someone was shouting. Someone was singing. And there were morning smells, too—hot cooking oil, bread baking, and underneath it all the stink of fresh poop.

An alley cut through the slum. Little paths wiggled out from it in random directions. Open sewers, filled with brown swill, lined every path. Cardboard shacks and broken huts held together with plastic sheets, black tarpaper, bits of wood, old tires, and chipped shingles retrieved from the dump surrounded the orphanage.

The wooden porch wrapped around the Pink House, all the planks were in different stages of rot. A small kerosene lamp sat on a three-legged stool beside Bell's rocking chair. The chair was fastened to the floor with a black chain.

Pax pulled the stool closer. He was holding a length of thread and a needle. First he wet the tip of the thread with his tongue, then he held the needle up to the light and slipped the thread through its eye. He stabbed the needle and thread into his old blue school shorts. Pax was almost eleven years old, and Kai was three. The shorts were too small for him and too big for Kai. Cutting the shorts down to fit Kai without scissors would take some ingenuity. Pax needed new shorts for school, but how to tell Bell?

"I am awake!" Kai announced from the doorway. He flung out his arms, as much to announce his presence as to greet the day. He was a strong little fellow with big eyes, a big grin, and black, stiff hair.

"It's too early, go back to sleep." Pax pulled the thread through the elastic waistband.

"But the sun is up." Kai kneeled beside Pax. The sun was not up, although the pinhole of light had expanded into the shape of a lemon.

"You can sleep a little while more," said Pax. He pricked his finger and sucked up the spot of blood.

"No, tell me again." Kai plopped down beside him and looked up at Pax with eyes as big as pies.

"I've told you a million times." Pax broke off the thread with his teeth and tied it off with a knot. "Try these on and see if they fit." He held out the blue school shorts.

Kai kicked off his brown shorts, stood bum-naked on the porch, and pulled up Pax's old shorts. "Now I can go to school," Kai announced.

"You have to be six to go to school. Do they fit?" Pax tilted his head and tried to judge for himself. Kai let go. The shorts fell down. Pax sighed. This wasn't going to work.

"Please, please tell me." Kai pulled on his old brown shorts, sat beside Pax, hugged his knees into his chest, and leaned his head against Pax's shoulder. "Please, please, please?"

"One last time," said Pax, knowing full well that it would not be the last time. He threaded the needle again, and stabbed the shorts again.

"On a planet far away, past all the stars and heaven too, a beautiful queen had a baby. War came to the planet. The queen asked a magician to save her baby from the enemy." Pax sighed. He had told the tale so many times he was almost sorry he had invented it.

"What did the magician look like?" asked Kai.

"He had a long white beard and a blue hat. His wand was made of gold."

"Then what happened?" Kai covered up a yawn with his fist.

"The magician used his wand to create a rainbow. Ouch!" This time a great bubble of blood oozed out of his thumb. Pax plugged his mouth with his thumb and flung the shorts on the floor.

"Then what?" asked Kai.

"The queen put the baby on the rainbow and the baby slid down to earth." Maybe Mega could help with the shorts.

"You forgot to say that *I* was the baby," said Kai.

"The baby's name was Kai," added Pax.

"Then what happened?"

"I caught you." Pax looked up at the hole in the wooden awning that covered the porch. He'd found six straight, rusty nails at the dump the day before. But the house was rotting from the outside in and the inside out. Eventually the rot would meet, and then what? There was no money to fix anything properly. There was barely enough money for food.

"You did not *catch* me. You *saved* me," said Kai.

"No, I caught you," replied Pax.

"What color was the rainbow?"

"You know the answer—all colors," said Pax. Of course, the real problem was the ceiling inside the house.

"No, tell me," Kai pleaded.

"Blue and pink and orange." Pax poked the needle into the spool of thread. Needles were hard to come by.

"Did the queen love me?" asked Kai.

"Of course."

"Will I go back up the rainbow?" asked Kai.

"Everyone knows that you can slide down a rainbow but you can't climb back up," said Pax.

"Why not?" Kai yawned.

"Rainbows are slippery, and you must stay with me now," said Pax.

Kai nodded. It really was awfully early. He leaned against Pax and closed his eyes.

Chapter 3

"**P**ax, where are you? Come here, NOW!" Bell's voice rebounded off the walls and wafted out onto the porch.

"Kai, stay here." Pax gave Kai his best stern look. Kai was growing curious about the world beyond the Pink House, but there were dangers about—rats and stray dogs, most carrying diseases, and there were holes and ditches to fall into.

Kai nodded, his chin bouncing off his chest.

Pax extinguished the kerosene lamp and scrambled up. He walked through the pink great room. Bell called it that, although Pax never understood what was so *great* about it. Bits of things were scattered about: a broken table, rugs, thin blankets, worn pillows, and sleeping mats—all but his and Kai's were topped with a sleeping child. Not even Bell's bellow could wake them.

Pax walked around the edge of the room, his feet making soft *slap-slap* sounds on the floor. What was left of the pink floor paint had retreated to edges of the room.

11

Bell was in her office, which had doubled as her bedroom ever since the roof above her real bedroom had fallen in. He stood in the threshold. Bell always said that standing in a doorway brought bad luck. "In or out," she would say, waggling a finger. Today, she did not even notice him hovering there.

He could see tufts of gray hair bobbing above the stacks of papers piled on her desk. Bell's bed (she called it a *cot*) was behind the desk. To the right was a bookcase filled with fat, leathery books embossed with gold lettering—volumes of the *Encyclopedia Britannica*. There were also books on first aid, algebra, and taxidermy, *Mrs. Beeton's Book of Household Management*, and several on birds. On the bottom shelf were children's books: *Black Beauty, The Big Book of Fables, The Railway Children*, and little books about a rabbit named Peter and a man called Mr. McGregor. The books had arrived over the years in small, wooden crates sent by Bell's sister. Edible treats for the children often accompanied them, along with bubble-wrapped bottles of Camp Coffee for Bell.

"Bell, do you want me?" asked Pax.

"Why would I call you if I didn't want you? Look at this!" She waved a letter about like a little flag. She was still in her old, flowery nightdress. Her gray hair, bundled in the back, was a tangled mess.

When had she received a letter? He always brought in the mail himself, and there had not been a delivery in days. The King did not consider their district important enough for regular mail delivery. Besides, Bell seldom opened her mail unless there was a chance that it contained money.

"I found it under all this rubbish. It must have come weeks ago. It's from the agency. Peter is bringing an American woman to see the orphanage this morning. THIS MORNING! Wake the children." Bell was flustered.

"Peter?" Pax was confused.

"Dr. Bennett to you. He's not a doctor-doctor. He's an education specialist, but he has connections in the government. He can help us; he *has* helped us. Tell Cook to make a fruit plate, and coffee. Go."

Pax was thinking that it would be hard to tell Cook to do anything, since she wasn't paid very often. And he was pretty sure there was no coffee left, or fruit, aside from what the children would need for breakfast.

"But what about school?" he asked.

"No school today. Hurry up." Bell patted her hair, as if that would have any effect.

Pax nodded, although he did not understand.

"Oh, and keep Kai out of sight," Bell added. "A government official may tag along, one of those ridiculous women from Children's Services. Why don't they help the children living on the streets? Millions of them. Why bother us? Oh, never mind." She swished her hand in the air. "All the same, we don't need the government finding out that we took in a child against their stupid orders." Bell pursed her lips and shook her head. "Take him to Ol' May's hut. Tell her that I will give her a beer if she doesn't smack him. Don't stand there like an ornament. Go!" She pointed to the door.

"No, wait!" she yelled. Pax spun in a circle. "Line up the children on the porch. Tell Mega to put the ribbon in her hair.

How is it that we have only one girl in this house? Hurry, they could be here any minute. Close the door. No, never mind, I'll do it myself. WAIT! Tell the children to put on their school clothes. Spit spot. Look sharp."

"But you said that we are not going to—"

"GO!" Bell, as tall as a ten-year-old, hustled around her desk and slammed the only door in the house shut.

Pax took five long steps, stood in the middle of the great room, and called each child's name. "Bhima, Santoso, Guntur, Bambang, get up. Visitors are coming. Put on your school clothes." He tried to sound like Bell. "Spit spot," he added.

All four gave him sleepy, curious looks. It was a school day. What else would they wear?

"Where is Mega?" Pax asked but did not wait for an answer. He charged out to the porch.

"Kai, come here," Pax called out. Where was he? He called again, and again.

"Here I am! Catch me." Kai raced around from the back of the house, ran up the steps and, with a mighty leap, flung himself at Pax.

"Whoa!" Pax's arms circled the child as he stumbled backwards. Kai giggled.

"That wasn't funny. Where did you go?" Pax set him down and put his hands on his hips, which is exactly what Bell did when she was annoyed.

"The outhouse," said Kai. "Am I in trouble?"

Pax reached down and gave Kai's yellow T-shirt a tug. "Not yet. Just don't run off. You are a good boy." And Kai *was* a good boy. Pax saw to it.

"I have something to tell you." Kai stood on his tiptoes and cupped his hand around Pax's ear. "Mega lost her penis," he whispered.

"Her what?" Pax stepped back, amazed.

"I saw ... in the outhouse."

Just then, Bell emerged from her office like a tiny bull released from a stockade. "Pax, I told you to take Kai to Ol' May's. Hurry. They may be here any minute." She was wearing her least dirty dress. A dark stain, in the shape of a muddy flower, bloomed below her shoulder. The stem of the muddy flower trickled down to the hem. The washer-woman did not come very often, and like Cook, she had not been paid in months.

"Where is everyone?" Bell muttered something that sounded like *fuddy-well* and then went back in the house, presumably to make a search of her own.

"Guntur, Mega, Bhima, Santoso, Bambang," Pax yelled. Only Bambang made an immediate appearance. He tossed his head back and neighed like a horse.

Kai pulled Pax's shirt. "Pax, what about Mega's penis?"

"We'll talk about it later," whispered Pax.

"No, now! We have to look for it." Tears bubbled up, turning Kai's big eyes into puddles.

"Kai, go to Ol' May's house and wait." Pax gave him a nudge.

"No! Ol' May is mean and her head is big." He crossed his arms over his chest. Despite being only three, Kai spoke in complete sentences.

Pax nodded. Ol' May was scary looking. Only Bambang went near her, and that was because she paid him to do chores.

"I'll come and get you when the visitors leave. Be a good boy." Pax shooed him away. "Bambang, where is Cook?" he asked.

Bambang shrugged. "She did not come today."

"But I want to see the visitors too," Kai whined.

"What visitors?" asked Bambang.

"An American is coming to give us money," said Pax.

Bambang slapped his arms to his sides like a little soldier, then lifted one in a silly salute. "Tally-ho!" he hollered.

Pax rolled his eyes. Bambang was reading *Black Beauty* again. All week long he had insisted that he be called Merrylegs.

The others came after, each one seeming to emerge out of the woodwork. Mega, Bhima, Bambang, Santoso, and Guntur were all dressed for school, Mega in a blue skirt and white blouse, the boys in blue shorts and white shirts.

Santoso and Guntur, the twins, gave each other two swift punches.

"Stop that!" Pax got hold of Santoso's ear and gave it a twist. Santoso howled. Guntur gave his twin brother a smack for making a fuss. "Line up," Pax commanded. Five children were accounted for; he was the sixth. Pax did not count Kai.

"It's time to go to school," Bhima piped up. He was the smallest boy and normally as shy as Mega.

"We are not going to school," said Pax.

"But . . ." Guntur stopped punching Santoso.

"An American is coming. Neigh, neigh!" Bambang galloped up and down.

"There you all are." Bell pushed back the plastic door and

walked in front of the line, inspecting each child. "Bambang, pull in your stomach. You look too well fed. Mega, run and get that hair ribbon I bought for you. It is on my desk. Hurry. The rest of you, hold out your hands." Bell peered down at their nails.

Within minutes they were the best they could possibly be, under the circumstances. Mega returned with the ribbon laced through her fingers.

"Bell, Cook is not here," said Pax.

"Never mind, we can cook for ourselves," said Bell.

Pax lowered his head. Bell did not cook. What she was really saying was that he and Mega could cook for them all.

"Give me that." Bell tied the ribbon into a hank of Mega's hair. That's when Bell noticed Kai standing behind Pax. "Why is he still here?" She was fuming like a little smokestack.

"Kai, come. I will take you to Ol' May's hut." Pax reached out his hand.

"No." Kai jutted out his lower lip and crossed his arms over his chest.

It was too late anyway. The foreigners were coming up the path.

Chapter 4

A man and a woman jumped the ditch that ran beside the orphanage and stood on the porch. The woman wore jungle clothes: pants and a vest with many pockets, a hat with a wide brim (netting tucked around the crown), and a great big black purse-thing tied around her middle.

"Hello. Welcome to the Pink House," said Bell in the fake, cheery voice that she used for guests.

Introductions were made. The American woman spoke with an American accent, but the man Bell called Dr. Bennett spoke just like Bell. He was thin, with water-colored eyes.

Pax pulled Kai in close. "Just stay here and be quiet," he hissed.

"But Pax, what about Mega's penis?" Kai whispered.

Pax leaned down, cupped his hand around Kai's ear, and whispered, "Girls do not have penises. Only boys have penises. No talking."

The woman scanned the house, her eyes trailing up and

down, around and about. "It really is pink," she announced, her voice rising in surprise. She had a very long nose. Pax thought that she looked like a horse. He glanced at Bambang. Did he notice?

"We love the color pink," replied Bell with a snort.

Pax looked into Bell's eyes. This was no time for her to get . . . like she got . . .

Bell caught herself and cleared her throat.

"Bell, why don't you introduce the children?" Dr. Bennett interjected, quickly.

"The paint was a donation. Very kind." She coughed.

"Bell, introductions?" repeated Peter.

"Of course." Bell resumed her promenade behind the line of children. "This is Santoso and this is Guntur." She placed a hand on each of their heads. Both did their best not to twitch. "They are twelve-year-old twins—such good boys. They were babes, hardly walking, when a policeman brought them to me. He said that they had stolen fruit from a cart one too many times. They were starving, poor things."

Bell moved down the line. "This is Mega. She is ten years old."

Mega looked up at Bell, then over at Pax. She was eleven! Almost imperceptibly Pax looked at Mega and shook his head. Mega stayed quiet.

"When she arrived she was so frail that it would not have surprised me if she had floated away." Bell fluttered her fingers heavenward while moving sideways. "This is Bambang."

"No, Bell, my name is Merrylegs!" Bambang kicked up his legs like a pony.

Bell cleared her throat. "Yes, right, Merrylegs. He likes to . . . read . . . about . . ." Bell stopped and looked at the American woman. Did she know that she looked like a horse?

"He likes to read about *nature*." She moved on quickly and stood behind Bhima. "Ten years ago this . . . poor child . . ." she paused.

Pax sighed. She had forgotten his name again.

". . . arrived in the arms of a prison guard. This horrid man—quite filthy, actually—said, 'His mother is dead. If you don't want him, I'll take him back to prison.' What else could I do?" asked Bell. "They torture in prison. Everyone knows that."

Pax sucked in his breath. Would this woman report Bell for saying bad things about the King and his government? It was hard to tell.

Finally Bell stood behind Pax. "And this is my right-hand boy. His name is Pax, Paxton, and he came to us from a loving mother. She was very sick, but despite her illness, she took great pains to find her son a good home where he would receive an education. His father died before he was born." Bell gave Pax a little nod. She ignored Kai completely.

The American woman looked down her long nose at the orphans. Her eyebrows tented and her lips fluttered. The children smiled broadly. They knew from experience that any minute now the foreigner would reach into that big black thing around her waist and hand Bell coins. Only Pax knew that today Bell had higher hopes. If all went well—and so far, so good—the American would write a fat check, which was the same as money, or almost the same.

"Me, Bell! What about me?" Kai thumped his chest.

"And what is your name?" asked the horse-faced woman.

"My name is Kai." He beamed.

"And how old are you?" She bent down from the waist rather like a giant chair folding in half.

"I am THREE!" he replied proudly.

The woman straightened up, tilted her head, narrowed her eyes, and peered directly at Bell. "I don't understand. I thought all the children here were between ten and twelve years old?"

"He is visiting." Bell went from ruddy red to paper white.

"Bell, I know something!" Kai tugged Bell's dress.

"Later . . ." Bell peered at Pax, then shook her head, as if she were trying to get a bean out of her ear.

"What do you know?" The man with the water-colored eyes smiled at Kai.

Kai clasped his hands behind his back and took a deep breath. "I know that Bambang has a penis, Santoso has a penis, Guntur has a penis, but Mega does not have a penis because she is a girl." He took another breath. Bell looked as though she might say something, but Kai kept going. "And Bhima has a penis and Pax has a penis." Kai smiled. He looked at the man. "And you have a penis. And you . . ." Kai gazed up at the woman with the horse face who loomed over them all like a dark cloud. Her hair was tied up and tucked away. She wore no makeup.

Bell dropped her head. Pax held his breath. The rest of the children stared out towards the path, faces blank, eyes heavenward.

"You . . . have a penis!" Kai punched the air with his fist. He was triumphant.

No one spoke. Not a word. Even the morning sounds—birds, vendors, distant traffic, mothers bellowing at children—seemed to go mute.

"He's a very bright child. Unusual, really . . ." Bell's voice floated away.

Bambang couldn't help himself. He simply could not stand still any longer. He threw his head back, neighed, stomped his feet (hooves), and went galloping down the porch and into the house.

"I think we have heard enough." The woman pivoted on her heels and marched down the path.

Peter Bennett dug into his pocket and pulled out some bills. "We will talk later," he said to Bell in a whisper, their two heads almost touching.

Pax edged closer. He could hear everything.

"Thank you, Peter. I know you tried," said Bell.

"This is enough money for you to get by for the next few months. But Bell, the government is unstable." Peter slipped Bell the roll of paper money.

"I have been hearing about the revolt for years. I thought it would have died down by now, but the guns are getting closer," sighed Bell. There was no getting away from the sounds of a brewing civil war. At night they could hear gunfire. *Bam, bam, bam,* it pulsed like a hurried heart.

"Bell, none of us may be here much longer. Consider returning to England," said Peter.

"England? This is my home. I have spent my life here. I

know what they are saying. Orphanages are out of fashion. Am I supposed to spend my time looking for their relatives who do not exist? Perhaps I could place them in local houses so that they can be turned into servants. Is it better to leave them to the street? You all think that I am an old, white, imperialist colonist. I had no business coming here and picking up children like they were shiny stones. Well, it's too late now. I love them and they love me." Bell's voice, at first fierce, trailed away.

"Don't be so hard on yourself. You have given these children a home. And you are an orphanage in name only. You are a family. But the King and his henchmen are arresting people left and right. And the opposing bunch, who call themselves 'liberators,' aren't much better. They are a ragtag group, but they may yet become a force to be reckoned with." Peter spoke in a near-whisper, but Pax could hear quite clearly. Bell said that she loved them.

"Eventually they will come after foreigners. They'll make life unbearable for all of us."

"But you still have contacts in the government, correct?" asked Bell. Fear crept into her voice.

"I don't think we can count on anyone."

"We will get by." Bell stood firm, but she sounded tired.

Peter nodded in Kai's direction. "He speaks like a six-year-old."

"He can read, too." Pax's interruption startled Bell. She glared at the boy.

"Can he? So he does live here. I thought there was an understanding, Bell. No new children. I can't protect you if you break the rules." Dr. Peter Bennett did not speak harshly or rudely. There may even have been a small smile on his lips. It was hard for Pax to tell.

Bell looked as though she might say something, but then seemed to change her mind. The horsey woman was waiting down the path. "You had better go," she said.

Dr. Bennett nodded, hopped the ditch, and followed the woman down the path towards the main road.

"Now, where do I start with you lot?" Bell looked at Pax. "Isn't it bad enough that we have one child who thinks he is a horse? You are the one I trust, but did you take this child to Ol' May's when I asked you? No. And then you brag about him!" Bell turned away from Pax, bent forward, put her hands on her knees, and stared into Kai's very large brown eyes. "As for you . . ." She paused. Her lips flapped, and her jaw went up and down, but words did not come out.

Finally she stood up straight, sighed, and said, "Pax, put this money in the money box. Take out enough to buy yourself a pair of shorts for school. Did you think I didn't notice? Kai needs shorts too. Go!" She dropped the bills into Pax's hand. "And take the penis counter with you!"

Chapter 5

Two years later

"Breakfast," Mega called out as she placed a bowl of fruit on a mat. Now thirteen and still very shy, she was in full control of the kitchen, having assumed the role of cook naturally. The other children pitched in.

"Eat up, you lot, or you will be late for school," Bell bellowed from the doorway of her office. But her bellow was no longer fierce and was often followed by a coughing fit. She was tired a great deal of the time now, too. And she was no longer round and soft; in fact, she was skinny.

"We are leaving, Bell," said Pax.

"Don't let the door hit you on the way out. AND SHOES!!!" Bell bellowed and waved at the same time.

Shoes. Each child sighed. Bell believed that children had to *learn* how to wear shoes. That is to say, the soles of one's feet, left to their own devices, would harden into thick, flat, black, leathery flippers without the experience of shoe-wearing. Given that Bell had ambitions for every child, the wearing of shoes was a necessity. But how to outfit children who insisted on growing? In the end, each child had a pair of slip-slidey, toe-numbing shoes that they wore down the path to school. But once out of sight of the Pink House, and Bell, the shoes were removed and fastened (by laces, string, or plastic-bag ties) to each child's waist.

One might imagine that owning shoes would be a status symbol. Quite the opposite. The sight of the children with shoes bouncing off their legs or backsides announced to the neighborhood that they were from the Pink House and therefore orphans. To be an orphan did not simply mean that one did not have parents, it also meant that a child had no older siblings, aunts, uncles, grandparents, cousins, second cousins, third, fourth, or fifth cousins. The children with the shoes tied to their bodies had *no one*. Children that unlucky were to be avoided at all costs.

Pax followed Santoso, Guntur, Mega, Bambang, and Bhima out of the house, across the ditch, and down the lane. Only Kai remained behind.

Pax called their area a *village*. Bell had an English word for it: *slum*. For a very long time he didn't know what that meant. She might have said *platypus* or *penguin* for all the meaning the word had to him. But then he'd looked up the word in one of the fat books on the shelf in Bell's office. "Slum—squalid, overcrowded, inhabited by very poor people. Hovel, rathole." He'd also looked up the word *village*: "larger than a hamlet and smaller than a town. Settlement."

"We do not live in a rathole, we live in a village," he

muttered as he stepped up his speed. Teacher would be angry if they were late.

Five-year-old Kai sat cross-legged on the floor of Bell's office, pencil in hand, looking pensive. "Bell, do you know that eight times eight equals sixty-four, but if you take sixty-four and divide it by four it's sixteen, and if you take sixteen and multiply it by four it's sixty-four again?" He looked pleased.

"I do now." Bell sighed. Pax had taught Kai a few simple additions, then subtractions. Kai had learned his multiplication tables on his own.

Kai jumped up and picked a red ribbon off Bell's desk.

"Don't touch that. It's for Mega. I traded a perfectly ugly pair of earrings my mother left me for that," snapped Bell.

Kai dropped the ribbon on the smokestack-high pile of files. All around the office, tiny mountains of papers threatened to topple and explode like child-sized volcanoes. Kai trailed his fingers over a mound of paper.

"Careful, I don't want them to fall and get mixed up," said Bell.

"Why?" asked Kai.

"Why? Why do all children ask 'why'? Because the forms tell whoever wants to read them how you arrived, how much you weighed, your birth mother's name, and as much as I know about your birth father," said Bell.

Kai pointed to a piece of paper with Pax's name. "What does it say?" Kai reached for the page.

"Give me that." Bell snatched it back.

"What do you say about me? How much did I weigh?" Kai asked.

"How would I know? I made that bit up," Bell growled.

"Who is *whoever*?" asked Kai.

"Whoever what?"

"You said whoever wants to read them. Is whoever a boy or a girl?" asked Kai.

"Sit." Her eyes drooped.

"Bell, are you sick again?"

"Who says I am sick? You are not a doctor—not yet." Bell looked down at the pages in front of her.

"It's all right, Bell. You don't have to tell whoever about my mother. I know all about her," said Kai.

"Is Pax still telling stories? Aren't you too old for stories?" Her voice was grizzly and low, as if she had sand at the back of her throat.

"No. Pax's stories are real." Kai was adamant.

Bell looked into Kai's big brown eyes. "We could put those eyes of yours on a poster. Maybe people would give us more money." She sighed.

"My mother the queen will give you money, maybe," said Kai.

Bell shook her head. "You are five years old, a big boy. You can go to school soon. It does no good to have such wild fantasies. I highly doubt that your mother is a princess."

"She is not a princess. She is a queen." Kai was indignant.

Bell went back to flipping through her papers. Kai looked over to a hand-woven basket filled with art supplies sent to them by Bell's sister. None of the children knew her name, but they all recognized the boxes when they arrived from England.

Kai picked up a bottle of glue. "Bell, why does the glue not stick to the inside of the bottle?"

Bell did not look up. "Ask Pax."

Kai nodded. Pax would know. "Bell, can blind people see in their dreams?"

"Yes." Bell was definite.

"But can they see colors? How would they know it was red or orange if they had never seen red or orange?"

"Ask Pax."

"If someone is blind and goes to heaven, will he see God?" asked Kai.

"No one is blind in heaven."

"Is everyone perfect in heaven?" Kai walked around to Bell's side of the desk and put his head on her shoulder.

"Yes."

"Are there sick people in heaven? Are there babies? Do the babies grow up and then stop growing before they get old?" Kai's questions rolled out.

Bell stared hard at Kai over her reading glasses. She said nothing.

"I know, I know. Ask Pax." Kai shrugged. "Bell, Santoso said that when I first came here, you didn't want me." Kai folded his arms on the desk and rested his chin on top.

Bell let out a long stream of air, rather like a balloon deflating. "You were tiny. I did not think that you would live, but Pax said that he would take care of you." Bell's face softened. She sat back and looked off into the distance, as though she was seeing something inside her head. "He fed you like you were a baby bird. He carried you on his back. The boys on the road made fun of him. He never paid them any mind until one boy called you a little monkey. I thought Pax was going to tear him to pieces." Bell laughed. "Never in my life have I seen a boy care for another living soul like he cared for you. It was enough to make one believe in destiny."

"What is destiny?"

"Fate." Bell looked at the mess of papers in front of her, pursed her lips, and furrowed her brow.

"I don't understand."

"You will. Go now, I am busy. I am an old, white, English colonist woman who must try and undo the damage I have apparently caused." Bell peered down at the numbers on the piece of paper.

"I don't understand," said Kai.

"Neither do I." Bell rubbed her face with her hands. Her voice was soft, like she was talking to an imaginary person.

"Bell, are there black womans in England?"

"Yes. Women, not womans."

"Are there brown women?"

"Of course."

"If a brown lady came to take care of us, would she be an old, white, English columnist woman too?"

At first—stunned silence. Then Bell lowered her head. Her body shivered, then quaked, then shook like jelly. She made noises, funny noises, hiccup noises. She fell back in her chair. A sound came up out of her throat and exploded into the air. She cupped her hands over her face and rocked back and forth.

Kai watched. Bell looked a little bit scary. He crept forward and reached up to Bell's face and peeled her fingers away from her eyes, one by one. "Bell, are you crying?" He asked. She shook her head.

"No, I am laughing. I don't think I have laughed in a long time. And it's *colonist* not *columnist*. Sit." She took a breath. "I have work to do!"

"What's that?"

"It doesn't matter." Bell wiped her tears and smiled.

"Do I matter?"

"You matter."

Kai nodded and looked down at the papers. "Bell, those numbers are wrong. It says eighteen plus fourteen equals thirty-four, but really it's thirty-two." Kai pointed to the sheet of paper on Bell's desk.

Bell sighed. "You might have said that this minus over here was a plus, then it would mean that we had money."

"I don't understand," said Kai.

"I don't understand many things either. If the riots would stop, the tourists would come back, the King and his government would have more money, and we would not always be broke."

"I still don't understand," he repeated.

"Sit."

Kai thumped down on the floor and pulled out the encyclopedias. He read about molten lava, grenades called potato mashers, a deaf piano player, and the rules of cricket.

After a while he pulled out the book called *Algebra*. He liked books that had numbers in them.

The sun was still high in the sky when Pax and the children returned from school. Bell and Kai heard Pax clomping around on the roof. Pax was always on the roof. No sooner had Pax patched one area than another spot opened up and leaked.

Kai jumped up and raced towards the door of Bell's office. "Stay off the roof, do you hear me?" snapped Bell.

"I promise." Kai nodded and crossed his fingers behind his back.

"I see you. Don't come running to me when you fall off and break your leg." Bell picked up a stack of bills and tossed them in the garbage.

"But Bell, if I broke my leg, I could not run—"

"Off you go. And no more stories about where you came from." She shooed him away with a flick of her wrist.

Kai ran out onto the porch. The awning over his head creaked. "Pax, what are you doing up there?" Kai leaned his back against the porch railing and looked up.

"I am fixing the roof."

"No you're not. I can see you. You are standing with your arms out. Are you trying to fly?"

"No, that would be silly. I am feeling the air."

"What does it feel like?"

"It feels clean," said Pax.

"Can I come up?" asked Kai.

"No. It's too dangerous. See those nails in the cup? Hand them up." Pax picked up his hammer, crawled to the edge of the roof, and peered down at the boy.

Kai stood on Bell's stool and passed Pax the cup that held the rusty nails.

"I know something," said Kai.

"What do you know?" Pax covered a stretch of roof with a piece of rubber and banged it into place.

"I know the real story about me."

"Tell me," said Pax.

"My mother the queen wanted me to go to another family but I hid behind a star and waited. When she wasn't looking, I jumped onto the rainbow and came to you."

Pax crawled to the edge of the roof and looked down. "That's right!" Then he fell back on his haunches and laughed.

Chapter 6

"**M**ake way, make way!" Bell came charging out of her office. She was heading to the outhouse, but between her and relief were children playing on the floor. "Make way!" she shouted.

Bell dodged, weaved, and, with a swipe of her arm, bashed back the plastic sheeting that covered the door. Then she thumped across the porch, took a sharp turn, and sped towards the outhouse. She was instantly out of sight.

Bell was shrinking. She slept much of the time, and when she wasn't sleeping, she would sit on the porch and stare out towards the great city that winked in the far, far distance.

Pax waited for Bell on the porch. He held a small, badly worn blanket. He wasn't worried about her. Why should he be? Bell was just tired. She needed rest. But, what if she was really sick? What would happen to them? No, he couldn't think like that. He would take care of her until she felt better.

Bell returned from the outhouse, dragging her feet up

the steps. "I could sit on the bloody pot all day and nothing comes out." It was as if she was talking to herself.

"Here, Bell." Pax put the blanket around Bell's shoulders.

Bell took his arm and leaned on him as they walked slowly across the great room. She stopped midway and gazed over at Bambang, Santoso, and Guntur, who were playing quietly in the corner. "It's not fair—how I get older and you children stay so young." Bell stopped to take a breath and rested her head on Pax's shoulder. She took a few steps forward, each one tentative, as if the floor might give way.

"I might have had my own children, had things turned out differently. I was to be married, back in England. He was a handsome boy. I was only nineteen when he died. It was a motorcycle accident. Just like that, he was gone." Bell lumbered on.

"Harry," said Pax.

"Yes, his name was Harry. I have told you all this before, haven't I?" said Bell. Pax nodded. "But you can tell me again."

"My sister told me to soldier on, buck up. I hated her for it. I was no beauty and I knew it. And I knew I'd never find another like my Harry. I was a widow without ever having been married. I left England on my twentieth birthday and haven't been back since." Bell stopped and looked down. "Oh, I am sorry." A puddle formed around her feet.

"It's all right, Bell, I will clean it up," said Pax.

Bell nodded. Gingerly, Bell clinging tightly to Pax's arm, they shuffled around the pee and reached her office. With a deep sigh, Bell lay down on her cot. "I will be better tomorrow. Visitors are coming tomorrow," she said as she closed her eyes. "Pax, are you still there?"

"I am here, Bell." Pax tucked the blanket around her thin, little body.

"Don't forget about the visitors." Bell took a deep breath. "'Every bad day has an end, and every good day has a beginning.' Someone said that. I wonder who? I suppose it's all been said and done before."

The visitors arrived at midday. Three men and two women picked their way carefully down the path, jumped the ditch, and climbed up the broken steps to the porch. One woman, wearing men's pants, looked angry and disapproving. The second woman wore a prim hat with a brim, a dress that swished and flowed around her like water in a pool, and shoes with little heels that left tiny tracks in the mud.

The man, holding a briefcase and looking very damp, asked to see Bell. Pretty Mega, with a red bow holding back her black hair, took them through the pink great room to Bell's office.

Only the man at the end of the line stopped to say hello to the children. Two years had passed, but Pax recognized him. It was Dr. Peter Bennett. Pax was sure of it. He was a doctor, but not a medical doctor. What had Bell called him? He could not remember.

Bambang, Bhima, and Santoso stood silently. Guntur licked his lips. Guntur was hoping for money, or at the very least candy.

"Kai, stand behind me," Pax whispered. He knew to keep Kai out of sight.

The children followed the visitors as they crossed the great room. Bell was stationed behind her desk, her fingers laced. She looked up from her desk, but instead of greeting them with a smile, she pursed her lips.

Today was one of Bell's good days. They came like that—a good day, followed by a bad day, followed by a good day. There were times when she seemed almost well.

The foreigners crowded into Bell's messy office. "Close the door, Mega," said Bell.

Later, the foreigners came out holding white cloths over their noses. Poor Bell was very stinky now. It wasn't her fault. It was hard keeping clean.

All but Dr. Bennett and the woman with the heeled shoes walked through the great room, across the porch, down the steps, and weaved carefully along the path towards the main road. No one said good-bye to the children.

"Is that him?" Dr. Bennett spoke to Bell but pointed towards Kai. Bell nodded.

Pax stood still. What did this man want with Kai?

"Pax, come here." Bell motioned to Pax. "Do you remember meeting Dr. Peter Bennett? He is an education specialist from England. He wants to speak to Kai for a moment."

Before Pax could open his mouth, Dr. Bennett bent down and said to Kai, "I hear that you like arithmetic, and you can read and write, too. I'd like to talk to you. Would that be all right?" He spoke kindly. Kai beamed and nodded.

Pax went out onto the porch and sat on the steps, resting his chin in his cupped hands. What would an educational specialist (whatever that was) want with Kai? Bell should have told him about Dr. Bennett. He was the one who cared most about Kai. Bell had no right, none at all.

Bell came out and sat on the stool. The woman with the hat sat in the rocking chair. Taking a fan from her purse, the woman rocked and fanned, rocked and fanned. The children—Mega, Bambang, Bhima, Santoso, and Guntur—sat around them and pretended not to listen.

"Well, Millie—may I call you Millie?" asked Bell. "What is it you young people say? Are you and Peter . . . involved?"

The woman called Millie laughed, and the children reared back in amazement. Millie had silver stuck in her teeth.

"Good grief, no. I am a volunteer. Peter is married to an academic—you know, the Oxford University type, all flat shoes and no lipstick. I have heard that she's mad for science and math. And she has a foreign name. Nadia, I think." Millie shook her head.

"Nadia is not an especially foreign name," said Bell.

"Well it's not Debbie or Susan, or something normal." Millie was miffed.

"His name is Bhima, and his name is Santoso." Bell pointed to the children.

"Well of course *they* would have foreign names. They *are* foreign!" said Millie.

Bell snorted as Millie fanned herself. The silence seemed to bother Millie. She wiggled about in Bell's rocking chair.

"I am sorry that it had to come to this. How many are left, ten?" asked Millie.

"Six," said Bell. She never counted Kai.

"Well, that's hardly an orphanage, now, is it? And it has been proven that orphanages are not the best places for children to grow up in." Millie bobbed her head as if to agree with herself.

"The government calls us an orphanage. I think of it as our home." Bell was weary.

"And the children can all be easily placed. Maybe the older ones can be put out to work. That's not unusual for this country. And with the government in another uproar, it might be a good thing to see them placed, perhaps in apprenticeships. They can't go to school forever," added Millie.

Bell said nothing. She looked out into the distance like a blind person.

"You must miss England after all this time. Think of the medical care that you will receive. Is there someone you can move in with?" Millie's voice pitched up into a whine.

"I have a sister. She has no soul. I can't possibly live with such a person," said Bell.

"Really, you don't mean that. When was the last time you saw her?"

"Thirty-five years ago. Just yesterday," replied Bell.

"People change." Millie fanned her face so hard that she created a small breeze.

"Do they? Or do they become more of what they really are? She called my work meaningless, as if living in a four-bedroom house with two cars in the drive gives her life meaning. Three and a half decades is still not long enough."

"Well, it's good to know that you stay in contact." Millie kept looking over her shoulder towards the door, or rather the plastic sheeting over the doorway.

"Yes, I get the occasional epistle, along with a packet of biscuits and a bottle of Camp Coffee," said Bell.

Pax listened to every word. He didn't understand *four bedrooms* or *two cars in the drive* or *epistle*. What he did hear was something about the children being *put out to work*. What did that mean? They all worked. He looked at Bell. She was struggling to sit upright. If only she were in the rocking chair and not perched on a stool. Bell's face had turned gray. He'd have felt sorry for her if he hadn't still been angry.

Just as Pax was about to go and check on Kai, Dr. Bennett sauntered out onto the porch, Kai behind jumping around him like a puppy.

"I will report back to you, Bell, but yes, you are right." Dr. Bennett motioned towards Kai.

Pax watched his every move. What did he mean? Right about what?

"Then you can make arrangements for him?" asked Bell.

"I will look into it. He will have to take more formal tests, but I have no doubt that he will do very well. He is an unusual boy. Think of how many children like him we miss, who end up dying on the street." Dr. Bennett pressed his lips together and shook his head.

"Every child has value, not only the gifted," Bell snorted.

Pax looked from Bell to Dr. Bennett. What gift?

"Pax here can tell the best stories in the world," Bell said.

Pax's mouth flapped open in wonder. Bell always told him that he had too big an imagination.

"And Mega could be a great chef one day, if she had the chance," she added. Mega lowered her head.

"What about us, Bell?" Santoso and Guntur bounced up and down.

"Zookeepers," said Bell.

"Yay!" The twins leapt up in the air.

"And as for . . . Bhima, he could be a . . ." She paused.

"He could be an explorer," said Pax.

Bhima looked at Pax in surprise. Pax had no idea what Bhima could or could not do; he just did not want him to feel left out.

Dr. Bennett faced Pax. "Bell tells me that you have taken great care of Kai." Pax stepped back and stared at the doctor. "I am here to help Kai, and you too, if you will let me," he added.

What was he to say? Pax didn't want any help. He looked down at his feet.

"We must be off. Dr. Bennett is leaving for London tonight," announced Millie as she stood, tucked her fan into her purse, and flicked imaginary dirt into the air.

"Wait, take a picture of us." Bell pulled a small box from her pocket and handed it to Peter. "Okay, everyone, get in line." Bell waved her arms about as though she were herding animals. "Mega, smile a little. Pax, you are the tallest, stand beside me. Kai, stand in front of Pax. Bambang, stop fooling around, you are not a horse. You should be over that by now.

And Bhima, straighten your shoulders and pull your shirt down. No one needs to see your belly." Bell arranged them in a line and then stood in the middle. Santoso and Guntur stood at either end like two anchors.

"Ready? Say cheese," said Dr. Bennett as he clicked the camera. None of them had ever eaten cheese, but they all knew the expression. "One more, just in case," and he clicked it again. "There you go, Bell." Dr. Bennett held out the camera.

"You keep it," said Bell with a flick of her wrist.

"I can't take your camera!" He looked confused.

"It's too far to go to develop the pictures. Take it." Bell waved him away as if he were one of the children.

"I will develop them for you and mail them to you at your London address. Someone will be in touch about Kai. I am sorry about all this, Bell, but you must think of your health now. You have done your bit." Dr. Bennett slipped the camera into his pocket.

To Pax, every word felt like a little spark that went off in his head. London? Health? Pax stared at Bell. She caught his eye, then turned away.

Dr. Bennett gazed at the small band of children. "I want to give you something. My brother sent it to me, but I think you, and your friends, might enjoy it." He pulled a book from his black bag and handed it to Kai. "It is called *The Seven Natural Wonders of the World*. When my brother and I were boys, we planned to see all seven."

"Say thank you," said Bell.

"Thank you," repeated Kai. He fell on his knees and opened the book on the floor. All the children gathered around.

Pax fixed his eyes on Dr. Bennett. He looked like a good man, but still, Bell should have talked to him before he spoke to Kai.

Millie stood behind Dr. Bennett looking bored. "Really, Dr. Bennett, don't you think that's a bit much? They will ruin it," she said.

"Nonsense. There are plenty of fine books here. And if they do, well, let's hope they have a good time ruining it." Dr. Bennett turned and waved. "Good-bye, Bell. We will catch up in England."

"Tomorrow is another day. A door closes and a window opens," added Millie.

Pax held his breath. Bell looked as if she might eat Millie.

Dr. Bennett and Millie set off down the steps and easily hopped the ditch.

"Bell, are you going to England?" Pax's heart was beating hard.

"It's too late for that," she said simply.

"But what did that woman mean when she said 'Tomorrow is another day'?" asked Pax.

"It means that she is an idiot."

Pax stood beside Bell and watched as Millie, halfway down the path, tried to scrape poop off her shoe. Unsuccessful, she carried on, tiptoeing down the path, her white hankie pressed to her lips.

"We are asked to forgive the fools of this world. I am tired of forgiving," whispered Bell.

Chapter 7

"Read it to us. Please, Bell, please Bell." Kai held the book up over his head. It was heavy and might have toppled him had Bambang not plucked it from his hands. "Please, Bell." Kai was relentless.

"You can read, can you not?" With the exception of Pax, Kai was the best reader of all the children.

"But it's better if you read to us," said Mega in a tiny voice.

"Bell must go and lie down," said Pax. Bell's face had gone from gray to white. Every breath she took seemed to be labored.

"Sleeping can wait." Bell lowered her tiny body into the rocking chair and read the title out loud. "*The Seven Natural Wonders of the World.* You know that there are also Ancient Wonders and Modern Wonders . . ."

The children did not know and they did not care. "Open it, Bell." Their voices blended into one.

"You sound like a Greek chorus." She turned the page.

"This is Mount Everest. This is the tallest mountain in the world."

The children puckered their mouths in *ooohs* and *aaahs*.

"Can people climb to the top?" asked Mega.

"They do it all the time and leave their garbage behind. Why climb a mountain? What good does it do? If one wants to do something hard, why not cure something? Leprosy, perhaps."

"Are there leopards on Mount Everest?" asked Guntur.

"I have no idea." Bell turned the page. "Here's another natural wonder, the Great Barrier Reef. That's off the coast of Australia. I think people are trying to poison it."

"Why?" asked the chorus.

"Because people are stupid," said Bell.

"Is it far? Can we go?" asked Santoso.

"Yes, and no," said Bell.

"What color is that?" Mega pointed to the picture.

"Blue. That is the color water is supposed to be," said Bell.

They could all see the ditch. Some days it was a trickle of sludge, but when the rains came, it was a bubbling stew transporting plastic bags, bits of rubber, cans. There were dead things, too—rats usually, or parts of things, a hoof or a paw. The color of the water was always the same—brown. Even the water that came out of the cistern in the kitchen was brown.

Bell turned the page. "This is the Grand Canyon. It's in America. It's a giant red ditch."

"It's beautiful," whispered Mega as she looked at the picture of red cliffs.

"It's a beautiful ditch." Bell huffed and scratched at the same time.

"Can people go there?" asked Bambang.

"Of course," said Bell.

"Will it still be there when I am older?" asked Kai.

"I'm guessing that it will be there when you get around to it. It says here that it is two billion years old or so," said Bell.

"It's older than you, isn't it, Bell?" asked Kai.

Bell stared hard at Kai. "And to think that you are my smart one. Here, take the book and go through the pages yourself. Pax is right. I must lie down now." Bell handed the book over to Mega, eased herself out of the chair, and slowly walked through the pink room towards her little office.

Mega, Bambang, Kai, Bhima, Santoso, and Guntur placed the book on a mat and turned each page with great care and reverence. Pax was not interested. Fear was crawling up his back.

Pax stood on the threshold of Bell's office.

"Come in or go out, but don't stand there like an empty bottle," said Bell as she flopped down on her cot.

"What did the man want with Kai?" Pax asked.

"Dr. Bennett gave him tests. Apparently we have a genius among us." Bell tipped a bottle of pills into a cupped hand and tossed the pills into her mouth as if they were nuts. She gulped water, then licked her lips.

"What does it mean—*genius*?" asked Pax.

Bell laid her head down on the pillow. "It means that one day Kai might get into a very good university."

"Like Oxford University, in England?" asked Pax. What had that woman Millie said? *An academic, the Oxford University type.*

"There are other countries that have excellent universities: Holland, France, America. What about the entire continent of Africa? What about South America? I'm sick of the assumption that only Western universities have any value. Why England?" Bell put her fingertips on her temples and rubbed.

"Because it's where you come from," said Pax, but quietly, almost in a whisper. Anyway, he didn't know what *assumption* meant.

Bell let out a sigh. "Kai is very young. It is all a long time away."

"Oxford University," repeated Pax. "Does Oxford cost a great deal of money?"

"Pax, enough. You are a dreamer. There are many good universities not far from here. And, with a few exceptions, all universities cost something. Get out the money box. At least we got some cash out of them." Bell pulled a wad of bills out of her pocket.

Pax rolled back the rug, pulled up a floorboard, and reached down for a rusted, tin money box. He put it on Bell's desk.

"Open it up," she said.

The hinges creaked as he pulled off the lid. Pax looked at the flat piles of bills held together by elastic bands. Some were multicolored and dirty, others were crisp and colorful.

The American bills were all green and hard to tell apart. Bell tossed in the new roll of money.

"How much is in here?" asked Pax as he poked the bills in the box with one finger.

"Not enough. All that money would not last a week in America or England." Bell closed her eyes.

"How much money does it cost to go to Oxford University?" He stood as if both feet were glued to the floor.

Bell opened her eyes and stared hard at Pax. "Ten times that amount just for travel, but after that, if he passed the tests, won a scholarship, and studied hard, he would have his tuition paid."

Pax repeated the word. "*Too-wish-on*. What is that?"

"It is the fee a student pays to go to university. Put the box away." Bell wiped her brow with the back of her hand.

Pax put the money box back in its hiding place, then pushed back the floorboard and rug. "Bell?"

"WHAT NOW?"

"Why did they come here in the first place? The foreigners, I mean."

Bell took a deep breath, then let the air out of her lungs slowly. "I suppose it's time to tell you. They want you all to be placed in a new facility, and then they will close this place down."

"What is a *facility*?" His heart pounded inside his chest.

"It is a building, a holding tank." Bell's voice was low, controlled, tired.

Pax shook his head. Water was held in tanks. Petrol was held in tanks. "But Kai and I will stay together?" Pax meant it as a statement, a conclusion, a fact, but it came out as a question.

"The government wants to clean up the streets. They want to show the world that there are no problems here, no slums, no orphans, no poverty," said Bell.

"We can all stay here together. I can work. I can shine shoes." Pax's voice shook.

"We haven't the money to keep this place open and I will not allow you to live on the streets. There are diseases on the streets, and drugs, not to mention the gangs. Out there, children younger than you will steal the clothes off your back—WHILE YOU SLEEP." She breathed deeply. "Everything I have done has been to keep you all off the streets. Five-year-olds work the streets. First they beg, and not long after that, they sell. And do you know what they sell? Themselves! You will all be educated at this *facility*. You could go to medical school and become a doctor, or maybe an engineer. Anyway, it's all been arranged." Bell swung her legs over the side of the cot and stood up. Beads of sweat crested on her forehead.

"But what you mean is that Kai will go to a different school from me, and that we will live in different places. We will be separated. Kai will be scared." Pax wanted to yell, to shout, *This isn't fair!* Instead, he pressed his lips together so tightly they lost their color.

"Listen to me, I was wrong. I raised you like British children. I protected you. No, I overprotected you. And that's what you have done to Kai. Kids his age are out working. He can read and write, he may be a genius, but how will that keep him alive? None of you would last a month out on the streets."

"We are not stupid." Pax just stood, shaking.

"I am aware of that. Tell me something, why did you take care of Kai? Why not one of the other children?" asked Bell.

"I do take care of the others." He was indignant.

Bell put up her hand to stop him. "It's different and you know it. I will tell you why. You recognized yourself in him. You want him to have what you did not. You want to raise yourself. But you are a boy too. You have great gifts. You have a purpose. Do you know why I named you after my father, Paxton John?" Bell did not wait for an answer. "I love all the children, but you are like my son."

Pax looked up, more shocked than surprised. She said it once before. He remembered, but he did not really believe it. She cared about them, fed them . . . but love?

"Feed the children their evening meal and leave me alone. Do not disturb me tonight," she said.

Pax turned and walked towards the door. Tears crawled up his throat and stung his eyes.

"Pax, wait!" Bell's face sagged, her eyes softened. "Remember what I said. It's time that you took care of yourself. 'Too long a sacrifice can make a stone of the heart,'" she whispered.

"I don't understand," said Pax.

"Those are the last words my sister said to me before I got on the airplane to come here. She couldn't even make up her own words; she quoted a dead poet. Go now. I am tired."

"Bell, do you have a stone in your heart?" Confusion was replacing anger.

Bell didn't answer. She thumped down in her chair, crossed her arms on the desk, and lowered her head.

Chapter 8

Nothing seemed right the next morning. The sun was behind a haze, the water in the cistern had turned from brown to black, twins Santoso and Guntur fought over a pencil and ended up breaking it in half, and Bell would not open her door.

"Pax, come. Bell is locked in her office," said Mega.

Pax cut up a mango and a banana and put them in a big dish for the children's breakfast. "Leave her. She is just sleeping. She did not look good yesterday. Get ready for school. Kai, come with us. Bell is tired."

Off they went, one after another. Partway down the road, Pax looked back at the Pink House.

"Pax, should we go back?" asked Mega.

Pax shook his head. "She just had one of her bad days yesterday. She will be better later today." He walked on but glanced back again, hoping to see Bell on the porch.

Hours later, when school was over, Mega raced ahead of all the children, bounded up the steps of the Pink House, flew across the great room, and knocked again on Bell's office door.

"Bell? Bell?" she called. Nothing, no answer. Mega put her ear against the wood and listened. Still nothing. "Pax, Bell will not open the door. She did not even yell at me to go away. Come, you wake her up."

"Bell. Bell." Pax hammered the door. He twisted the doorknob. It was made of tin and squeaked almost as loudly as Bell could yell. Locked. "Bell, open the door," Pax shouted. He looked down at his feet. "What's this?" He picked up an envelope. It had his name on the front.

"There is tape on it. Maybe it fell off the door?" said Mega. Pax ripped open the envelope and pulled out a piece of paper as Mega rattled the handle.

"Pax, there is no key. What should we do?" asked Mega.

"Go," he said.

"Go where?" Mega stared at Pax.

"Take everyone out to the porch. Sit with them."

Mega was a good girl, a quiet girl, and she was used to doing what she was asked. Today was no different. She told the children to follow her and, by some miracle, they did.

The paper read, "Do not open the door. Fetch the police."

Pax dropped it as he kicked open the door. It was flimsy, the wood rotten, the hinge rusted. It swung open easily and smacked into the wall. Bell lay on her cot, her arms by her side, her legs straight as wooden posts.

Startled by the noise, the children raced back across the great room and stood in the doorway of Bell's office, mouths agape.

"Go back. Go, go!" Pax waved them away and pushed the damaged door closed.

He knelt down and brushed the strands of silver hair from Bell's face. She was cold and her skin was paper thin. It was not Bell, not the Bell he knew. It was just an empty body, like the empty pill bottle beside her.

"Bell, Bell," he whispered. Tears rushed up the back of his throat. He might cry or he might be sick, he couldn't tell. The day was hot, but still he took the blanket, laid it across her face and down her body, then tucked it around her. It seemed like the right thing to do.

What should he do next? Bell's note had said to call the police. He would send Guntur to Ol' May's shack. She would know how to summon them. He moved about without thinking, as if he were a puppet controlled by invisible strings.

Pax looked at the papers on Bell's desk. Never, not once, had he seen the desk this tidy. Behind it was a garbage bag filled with paper torn into tiny bits.

Two envelopes lay side by side on the desk, one fatter than the other. They were both addressed to Children's Services. Pax opened the fat envelope. One page had the name of a school, and under it a list of names: Mega, Santoso, Guntur, Bambang, Bhima, and his own name—Paxton.

Official forms filled up the envelope, with detailed information for each child. They listed birth date, place of birth, weight at birth, parents' names. And then there was information about each child's education and medical history. Page after page. He came to the last page, the one with his name on it.

Bell's handwriting was feathery, the letters round and bold. Pax read: "Paxton John, three to four months, was discovered in a garbage dump. He was found by a rag-picker and arrived with multiple sores, weighing approximately . . ."

Pax stopped reading. Bell had lied to him. He had not been given away by a loving mother to a good home where he would get an education. He had not even been simply abandoned. He had been thrown out, like garbage. Left to die. He felt a blow to his chest, like a punch. He took deep breaths, one after another, clenched his fists and squeezed his eyes tight, tighter. Urgency pushed him on. He opened his eyes and sifted through the papers one more time.

Kai's name was not there.

Pax reached for the second envelope. His hand trembled. Inside was another official form, with the name of another school, followed by Kai's name. Pax looked down at Bell's body. Her last act on earth had been to betray him. She would have separated them.

Pax acted suddenly. He tore the form that had Kai's name on it into tiny bits. Then he took his own pages from the other envelope and tore them into pieces. He stood at the window and scattered them all in the ditch below. They mingled and floated on the water's surface like little stars.

"I beat you, Bell," he muttered. Now, neither he nor Kai existed.

Word of Bell's death spread through the slum like fire; Ol' May, the neighbor, saw to it. The police came. A doctor came. The doctor looked at the pill bottle. Everyone paid special attention because Bell was a foreigner. They didn't want any trouble with foreign governments. "Cancer medication." The doctor tucked the bottle into his pocket. Men wearing paper masks put Bell into a black zippered bag and carried her away. All this happened quickly. A body left too long in the heat would turn sour quickly. And then disease would come. All the children knew that.

"What will happen to her . . . to her body?" Pax asked a man wearing a mask and holding a clipboard.

The man shrugged. "What does it matter? She is a foreigner. Maybe she will go back to where she belongs."

Once their job was done, the workers left.

"What do we do now, Pax?" whispered Mega. The children huddled in the middle of the pink room.

"I am thinking," said Pax.

Mega sobbed. Kai clung to Pax's leg. Snot ran out of Bhima's nose, and he smeared it across his cheek with his fist. Bambang was stone silent. The twins looked off into the distance with wet eyes.

Eventually they dragged themselves up and did a few chores. Bhima swept the porch while Bambang shook the dust out of a small rug. Mega picked the ants out of the rice and Pax cooked it up. The children gathered around and ate out of a communal bowl in silence. When they were done, Pax spoke.

"I will finish the roof. The rains are coming. Kai, do as Mega says. The rest of you, go and wash."

Pax climbed up on the roof. He needed to be alone. He was not very high up, but on the roof the air seemed to smell better. The sun seemed closer and the birds friendlier. Here he could think—usually.

In one hand Pax held the nails and in the other hand a hammer, although he had no intention of using either. His shoulders sagged. His breath was short, his throat tightened. Then came angry tears. How do you yell at a dead person? "Why did you do this to us, Bell? We need to stay together!" He slammed his fist on the roof.

He looked up and saw birds overhead. Their wings flapped in harmony; the sun's rays made their feathers sparkle. What would it be like to fly? To soar through clouds, to feel the wind rush past—that's what it must be like to be free.

Pax was still on the roof when he spotted a man and a woman coming towards the house. They carried files and clipboards and wore red-and-blue badges on their sleeves. Hunched over, he waited. They were out of view when they climbed the steps to the porch.

"Pax!" Mega cried from below.

Pax didn't answer. Instead he snatched up the hammer, crept across the roof, and peeled back a tile. If she heard the creaking up on the roof, Mega did not let on.

Through his peephole Pax could see Mega leading the two adults across the great room. They were going into Bell's office. Crouching, crawling, Pax made his way back across the roof and jumped down onto the porch.

"Pax!" Kai cried and ran to him. Instinctively, without even looking down, Pax pushed Kai behind him. One by one the children stood behind Pax.

"You children must be moved. We do not want any nonsense." The man came out of the house holding Bell's letter. His face was pinched, his mouth pulled tight, his shoulders hunched. The woman followed.

"We do not need you. We can take care of ourselves." Pax yelled louder than he meant to.

"You will all be taken to a good place. You have been provided for," the man said, without looking any of the children in the eyes.

"Go away!" Pax shrieked. He was still holding the hammer. Without thinking, without even realizing it, he raised it in the air. "Leave us alone!"

The two left, one scurrying after the other.

Chapter 9

"Pax, we should do something—for Bell."

Mega looked up at him, her eyes liquid, her face pale. Bambang and Guntur stood behind her, heads bobbing. He couldn't tell them about Bell's betrayal.

Pax shrugged. None of them had ever attended a funeral, although they had seen people pray over their dead. They sat on the floor in a circle.

"Should we hold hands?" asked Mega. Pax shrugged again. Shy Mega took charge. They held hands. "We should say something nice about Bell," she instructed.

"She read us good stories," said Bambang.

"She never hit us," said Guntur.

"Not even when we broke stuff," added Santoso.

"She loved us," said Kai.

Love? Pax stood up and walked towards the door.

"Where are you going?" Kai asked.

He didn't answer.

That night, Pax lay awake on his sleeping mat in the middle of the great room. The children, lying on their own mats, swirled around him like little fishes caught in a whirlpool. They had trouble settling down.

"Go to sleep. There is school tomorrow," whispered Pax.

"What if something happens?" asked Bambang.

"Nothing will happen. Sleep now," repeated Pax. But it was Pax who could not sleep. Bell had said that they would not be able to manage on their own. Why not? They did not need much. Bell was wrong.

It was Mega who started it. The crying. One after another joined in, sniffing, sobbing. "I want Bell to come back." Maybe it was Guntur who spoke, but it might have been any of them. Pax lay still, his body rigid.

Another hole had opened in the roof. Pax could see one, two, maybe three stars. He drifted off to sleep after the stars had disappeared, when the night was darkest. He awoke as the sun came up. He crept into Bell's office, dipped into the money box, and tiptoed out of the house.

The children woke to a breakfast of bread, rice, fruit, and beans. "Eat," said Pax. It was a feast! They picked at the food. "Eat!" Pax repeated. What did they want? He couldn't bring Bell back. Kai curled up into a ball. Bambang put his head in his hands and rocked on his bum.

Afterwards, Mega washed the pot in the dingy cistern water. "Maybe the government people will forget about us," she said. Her eyes were puffed up and red. "If Bell were here . . ."

"Bell is not here. Get ready for school." He didn't mean to sound so harsh, but what more could he do?

Later, when they were all home again, Pax went to the place where he could think—the roof. Kai, Mega, and the rest were below in the great room. Pax sat hugging his legs, his head bouncing off his knees. It would be good to hear Santoso and Guntur fight, he thought, or Bambang neigh like a horse. How could he care for them all? He and Kai could manage on their own, he was sure of that—there was enough cash in the money box to pay for school and uniforms for years. But what of the others? He had to do the right thing, but what was the right thing?

Pax pressed his palms into his eyes, wiped his tears, and looked out over the village. A new road circled it like a rope. Ugly as this place was, it was home.

He caught sight of something out of the corner of his eye. A car and a covered truck had pulled over on the main road. Pax shaded his eyes and squinted. It was rare for a vehicle to stop near their village. Soldiers wearing red-and-blue uniforms tumbled out of the back of the truck. It was hard to tell how many—maybe six or seven. Pax stood up. Two people got out of the car. Soldiers led the way. They were moving through the alley. They were coming directly towards the Pink House. Black clubs were clutched in the soldiers' hands.

"Kai!" Pax jumped off the roof and landed on the porch. "Kai!" he cried. With a sweep of his arm, Pax pushed aside the plastic sheet and ran into the great room.

Mega stood still, a pot in one hand, a stained towel in the other. Santoso and Guntur looked up from a book. Bambang and Bhima stopped playing with a coin in the corner. They stared at Pax.

"Where is he?" Pax was wide-eyed, frantic, his arms outstretched.

"What's the matter?" Mega held the towel to her mouth. The room vibrated with fear.

Pax ran towards Bell's office. Kai was sitting cross-legged on the floor. Pax pushed back the rug, pulled at the floorboards, and picked up the money box. "Come." He held the box under one arm and scooped up Kai with the other.

"Put me down!" Kai screamed. He flailed around, his arms and legs waving in all directions.

"Pax, what's wrong?" Mega was screaming too. Santoso, Guntur, Bambang, and Bhima stood frozen in place.

"Mega, it will be all right. They will take you to a school. You will all be together." Huffing, puffing, Pax headed for the door.

"Put me down!" Kai squealed like a little pig, pulled back, and wriggled out of Pax's arms.

"What's happening?" Mega was by Pax's side.

Pax dropped the money box and put his hands on Mega's shoulders. He looked at her, really looked, maybe for the first time. She was like his sister.

"Pax, please." Her voice was as tiny as her body. He could feel her shoulder blades under his fingers, sharp and as pronounced as wings. She looked at him with coal-black eyes, her stare piercing and trusting at the same time. For a moment Pax faltered. The moment passed.

"Listen, they will take Kai away from us—from me. I have to go. Stay with the others." He couldn't look at her any more. He was weakening. He might hug her. Instead, suddenly, he pushed her away. "Kai!" he cried as he reached down, picked up the money box, and took firm hold of the boy's arm.

"What do you mean? What school? Who will take us?" Guntur blocked Pax's way.

"The soldiers. Bell planned it. You must go with them. It will be all right. You will have each other." Pax used his shoulder to push Guntur aside.

"Where are you going?" Guntur yelled.

"Pax, don't leave us!" Mega reached out and grabbed Pax's shirt. She held on tight, her fingers threading through the material. "Please, Pax," she sobbed.

He turned and took one last look at Mega, at Santoso, at Bhima, then swooped down and picked up Kai.

"Let me down, let me go!" Kai cried.

Pax stumbled out onto the porch and down the steps. He fell into the ditch.

"Pax, you are hurting me," Kai cried.

"Quiet," whispered Pax. He scrambled up, shaking off the filth.

"Pax, come back!"

It was Mega's voice. He paused. The soldiers were shouting something. He cocked his ear like a dog. Holding

Kai in his arms, and with the money box clutched in his hand, Pax ran. As he turned down a laneway, he heard Bambang cry out, "Don't leave us!"

Pax tried to catch his breath. His head jerked from side to side. "Hide," he said, pushing Kai into a shed.

"What about Mega?" Kai sobbed.

"Shush," said Pax. He squatted on the money box, his body shielding Kai. Pax peered through a narrow slit in the shed wall. He could not see the others, but he could hear soldiers yelling commands.

"Pax?" Kai sobbed.

"Don't speak," Pax hissed.

They sat. Kai's legs were crammed in. Tears ran down his face in sheets. Only when Pax leaned forward could Kai look past him to the hole in the shed.

"Mega," he cried.

"Quiet!" said Pax. He could see her too. "They will be all right. They will be all right," Pax repeated. "They will go to a *facility*. They will be all right."

Kai sobbed into Pax's shoulder. People were yelling at the police. There were screams.

"Wait here. Wait!" Pax turned and looked Kai in the eyes. Kai nodded dumbly, his head bobbing.

Pax left Kai sitting on the money box as he climbed up onto the roof of the shed. He curled his toes around the peak of the roof and shielded his eyes with a cupped hand. The children were being herded in a line through a pathway. Crowds were forming on either side of the line. "Where are you taking them?" the people cried. "What do you want with our children?" It was a surprising thing to say, shocking even. No one had cared about them before. Why now?

The police waved their clubs in the air. "Get back!" they shouted at the growing crowd. Pax could see them all—Bambang, Bhima, Mega, Santoso, Guntur. Mega's head was bent, her hair falling over her face. Bhima shuffled behind her. And then Santoso and Guntur bolted and ran down an alley. Pax held his breath. Three soldiers split off from the group and chased after the two boys.

Pax stood up. He could see Santoso and Guntur weaving and dodging carts, boxes, people. Arms pumping, they raced towards the main road that circled the slum.

"No!" Pax screamed across the rooftops. A great bus with tinted windows was rounding a corner. "STOP!" How could the bus see them? "STOP!" he cried. Helpless, his arms outstretched, the cry caught in his throat, Pax watched as both boys rolled under the wheels of the bus.

"Pax!" Kai thumped at the side of the shed. Pax jumped down. He swung open the door, arms wide. Kai fell into them. "What happened?" Kai cried.

"Don't be scared. Listen to me. Don't be scared." Pax held Kai tight and rocked him. "I will take care of you. I won't let anything happen to you." Kai's tears wet Pax's shirt. "I will keep you safe. I promise. Forever."

Only when the sun began to set did Pax and Kai creep back to the Pink House. The porch was empty and the plastic door had been torn down leaving a gaping hole, like an open mouth with no teeth. Thieves had already stripped away what little they had. Bell's desk and rug had been taken. All the books and encyclopedias were gone, except for one volume, "Q-R-S." *The Seven Natural Wonders of the World* was missing too, but the book on algebra lay open on the floor, its spine broken, pages exposed.

Their own sleeping mats, pillows, even school uniforms were gone. Only a few dirty mats were left in the corner. The spices, a knife, spoons, and tea had been stolen. Kai picked up the damaged algebra book and hugged it to his chest. Pax picked up the encyclopedia.

That night, when Kai was asleep, Pax opened Bell's money box and divided the money into piles. He would save the foreign money. Bell had said that they would need ten times this amount to get to England. He would have to work hard, very hard, if Kai was going to go to school. "Ox-ford University, two-wish-on," he repeated over and over while rubbing his face with the back of his hand. He tucked the local, dirty bills into his pocket. This money would be used for food, rice and figs, and two new school uniforms.

Chapter 10

The sun poked in through the roof. No one had come back for Pax and Kai. But why should they? The authorities did not even know that he and Kai existed. Perhaps Dr. Bennett would remember Kai but he was in England. They were safe for the moment.

Pax heard cracking sounds—wood being snapped in half. Then came ripping sounds. Pax jumped up and ran out onto the porch.

"Hey, get away from here!" Men and boys, all holding hammers, were stripping the wood off the Pink House. It was disappearing, plank by plank. "Go away!" He waved his arms as if he were shooing away giant birds.

The men stopped. Some thumped their hammers in cupped hands, others ignored the two and got on with pulling down the house. "Get out before this place falls on your head," jeered a man as he walked towards Pax. He had a beard, long hair, and wore Western jeans.

"You have no right. This is private property," cried Pax as he puffed out his chest. His heart thumped and his legs quivered but he stood his ground.

"And who is going to stop us, you? Get away before you get hurt." The man curled his lips over his teeth.

"Pax, what are they doing?" Kai came up behind Pax and hid behind his legs.

"Stay back," Pax hissed.

"Pax, Pax," Ol' May yelled from beyond the ditch. "Come away from there." She motioned to Pax with a hand as big as a dustpan. Bell had said that Ol' May had a disease that made her hands and legs big—elephant big. Her head was big too, and her hair was wild, like a lion's.

Pax looked at the man eye to eye. He couldn't win, he wouldn't win. "Stay with me," he whispered to Kai.

Pax dashed back into the house, with Kai on his heels, and wrapped up the money box in the last, dirty mat. He tucked it under his arm. "Get your books." Pax tipped his head towards the two books on the floor.

"What are you doing?" whispered Kai.

"Stay close."

Pax stepped outside again and crossed the porch. The men had gone back to destroying the Pink House, their home.

The boys jumped the ditch and walked towards Ol' May.

"I knew you still here. Those men—bad men. Take." She held up a bowl of burnt rice. Pax clutched the mat and the money box tightly under his arm and peered, stone-faced, into the bowl. It was rice scraped from the bottom of a pot. A beetle, as fat as a finger, crawled across the crust. Dogs would not eat this stuff.

"You good boy. Bell always say, but she no friend of Ol' May. She say, 'Pax my best boy.' She thought she better than me. Fancy-pants, that what she was. I bet she named the lice that crawled over her. But she gone now, and she no coming back. You live with me. You do what Ol' May say. See, nice house." Ol' May pointed to a two-room shack that leaned in the direction of the vanishing Pink House. It was made mostly of old car tires. Plaster and mud held the tires in place. "Here, take." She shoved the bowl of rice into his chest.

"Thank you," Pax muttered. He nibbled at the rice. He could not admit that they had Bell's money box, and that they had enough money for food and had been eating every day.

"Speak up, boy. You no want to live with Ol' May? You can live on the road. I no care." She waved a fat hand.

He looked behind him. More boys had joined in to tear the wood from their home. At this rate the Pink House would collapse in a few hours.

Where could they go? He could rent out a bed maybe, in another place. But then the money would dwindle. It was best to spend the money on food and school. Ol' May would not charge them, but she would make them do chores. Pax knew what one of the chores would be. She paid Bambang a few coins to sweep her shack and empty her piss-pot every day. He pursed his lips, lowered his head, and considered. Lots of people lived on the streets. He could do it if he was on his own, but what would he do with Kai?

"Kai must stay too," Pax said.

"No, no. He too young. He bother. Take him to the church. Leave him on steps." She waved her big paw about.

"We stay together," Pax insisted.

"Go find somewhere else to live." Ol' May turned and flaunted her big backside. Pax knew the game. She was bluffing.

He looked up at her roof. "The rains are coming and your roof is leaking. I will fix your roof."

Ol' May turned back, twisted the hairs on her chin, and chewed her lower lip. "You fix the roof and stay one week. See that kid no cry," she said.

Pax agreed.

That night Pax listened to Ol' May's snoring. When he was sure that she was in a deep sleep, he crept across the floor, pulled up a floorboard, and lowered the money box into the hole. There was one place that Pax was positive Ol' May would never look—under her piss-pot.

Chapter 11

Every day Pax bought Kai meat and fruit. They walked far from Ol' May's shack because Pax did not want the neighbors to see that they had money. But how to explain their new sleeping mats, clothes, and notebooks?

"Bell left me this much." Pax held out his hand and revealed one piece of paper money and coins.

Ol' May's eyes brightened. She lifted her hand.

"No!" Pax snapped his fingers closed. "This is for school." Before Ol' May could lash out, Pax handed over three coins. "This is for you, because you are . . . nice." Pax grabbed Kai's hand and ran out the door.

They went to a new school on the other side of the village. No one knew them; no one asked questions. Teacher was kind. His skin was like copper shining in the sun. He did not have many teeth but the ones left in his head were very fine. He did not hit the boys too often. There were fifteen students of all ages, but no girls.

The schoolroom was a room in a house. A butcher shop was beside the house. All day butchers sliced meat from sheep carcasses that hung on hooks in the open air. The stench singed the insides of their noses.

The students sat cross-legged on woven mats that covered a cement floor. Pax was the oldest and Kai the youngest, although few boys knew their ages for certain.

Teacher read poetry out loud.

> The breeze at dawn has secrets to tell you.
> Don't go back to sleep.
> You must ask for what you really want.
> Don't go back to sleep.

"Pax, what does he mean?" whispered Kai.

"It means that if you want to ask God for help, you must be awake," Pax whispered back.

Later, on their walk back to Ol' May's, Kai announced that he could make a poem too.

"Only poets can make poems," said Pax.

"But I *will* write a poem." Kai picked up a stick and scratched words into the sandy road. The earth was hard and the marks just chicken scratches.

"Read it to me," said Pax.

Kai read:

> One hand holds back the ocean,
> The other hand holds back the wind.
> One hand sweeps away dirt,
> The other hand wipes away tears.

"Do you have four hands?" Pax asked.

Kai nodded. "See?" He pressed his palms against Pax's palms. "Now I have four hands." He giggled.

"And now you are a poet," said Pax.

Laughing, Kai swung on Pax's arm.

After the first week, Teacher did not ask Pax to pay Kai's school fees. Kai was his prize student. Teacher said that Kai was one of the smartest boys he had ever taught. "He can attend high school. He will make my little school famous." Teacher grinned a toothy grin.

"Class will begin," said Teacher as he tapped his desk with a pointer.

Two boys, sitting side by side at the back of the class, pushed one another. Teacher raised his voice. "Who started this?" he asked. Each boy blamed the other.

Teacher said, "God has knowledge of everything." He waited. The boys hung their heads. Teacher smiled. The other students grinned sheepish grins.

"Does God care about Pax and me?" Kai asked.

Teacher said, "If you need anything, pray to God and He will help you."

Kai's jaw dropped. He was amazed. "What do I say to God?" he asked.

"Whisper to God, and the whisper will return like a song," said Teacher. "Now we will return to mathematics."

After school, and with happy thoughts in his head, Kai hummed as they walked back to Ol' May's shack.

"Look, Pax." Kai noticed a poster tacked onto a wall in the alley. "Is it a bird?" he asked.

They both stared. The creature on the poster had a long, white, feathered tail speckled with glittering stones. Her body was birdlike but her face, sculpted as if in stone, was that of a beautiful girl. On her head was a crown of sparkling pebbles.

"What is it doing there?" asked Kai.

"I don't know," said Pax. There were no words on the poster—nothing.

"Can we take it?" Kai asked.

Pax looked up and down the street. No one was watching. He carefully peeled the poster off the wall.

The two boys ran into Ol' May 's hut. They put the poster up on the wall, then sat down on their mats and admired it.

"She is like a queen," said Kai.

"No, a goddess," said Pax.

Kai leaned against Pax. Teacher had said, "If you need anything, pray to God." What would he pray for? He did not like Ol' May, but he had a mat, and food, he went to school, and most of all he had Pax. He had everything he wanted.

Chapter 12

"Pax, it has been a year since you have been in my school. You are smart enough to go to a state school. I have taught you all I know," said Teacher.

Pax shook his head. "I must stay with Kai. He is only six," he said.

Teacher looked at Pax with soft eyes. "You are a good boy. If you stay, you can be my assistant and teach the younger ones."

He gave Pax a few coins to repeat the alphabet and numbers to young students. Every cent was accounted for, but he needed more money, much more money. He needed work.

There was a taxi stand on the main road. Pax and Kai passed the stand every day. A driver pulled Pax's arm. "I pay you ten cents for every fare you get for my taxi," he said. Pax agreed to come every day after school.

"Pax, I want to work too," said Kai.

Pax shook his head. He wanted to keep an eye on Kai. It was easy to lose sight of a small boy on a crowded street.

Kai squatted on his haunches in an alley between two shops and looked at the numbers in his copybook. Pax tried to get the attention of people walking by. It was hard work. He watched the other boys doing the same job. They cried out, "Hey Mister, you look rich. You should drive in a car like a rich man." Pax tried shouting too. "Take a taxi, Mister? Why walk?" It took Pax three hours to make thirty cents, only enough to buy rice and bread.

One day Pax made nothing at all. An older boy said, "There is a foreign man looking for bike couriers." Pax did not know what a bike courier was. "You ride a bicycle and deliver packages. And they even give you a bike," he said.

Pax made a deal with Ol' May. He would give her part of his pay if she would watch Kai. Ol' May agreed. Pax went off to become a bicycle-boy. That's when Pax met Andy.

Andy had red hair. He was a foreigner who came to their city to help street kids. Andy said that the deliveries were local and that the boys did not have to travel too far into the city.

The boys sat on wooden benches in an upstairs room of an old building and waited for the telephone to ring. Andy would call out a name and say something like, "You, go to Banboo Street and pick up a package. Ask for . . ." And then he'd say a name, like Mr. Samaur or Mr. Bitoo. When a bicycle-boy delivered the package, he usually got a tip. It was a good job, easy too, until the rains returned.

The rains began like silver threads dangling from the clouds. But soon the threads were so numerous and fell together so quickly that they became as thick as sheet metal. Dirt paths turned slimy and slippery. Ditches became swollen with water. The debris and sludge that clogged them began to run free and spilled over onto the paths and roads. Bike tires got caught in the little rivers. The bicycle-boys repeatedly tumbled over their handlebars and into the mud. Packages fell into the muck too. Some days they did not get a tip; they got a clip to the ear instead. Some days the telephone did not ring and the boys just sat, backs to the wall, waiting.

One day a man clomped up the stairs. He stood in the doorway and gazed around the room, resting his eyes on one boy, and then another, and then another. He looked at the boys as if he were inspecting fish or meat. He gave his closed umbrella a good shake and then flicked off rain that had beaded like tiny pearls on his suit. Thin as a stick, he walked past the boys and into Andy's office.

Andy had a window in his office door. No one could hear what the two were saying but Pax could see Andy frown, shake his head, and run his fingers through his red hair until it stood up in points, rooster fashion.

The man came out of Andy's office and stood at the top of the room. He pointed. His fingernails were curly and as brown as wood.

"Who would like to make a lot of money?" he asked.

Hands shot up in the air. "Me, me, me!" the boys cried.

Pax shoved his hands under his thighs, as if to pin them in place. There was something wrong about this man. But what?

The man's upper lip pulled into a sneer. He had stubby, yellow teeth, a forehead as slanted as a roof, and the eyes of a snake lying on a hot rock. Even from where Pax sat on his bench, the man smelled stale, like water in the ditch.

"They call him Mister," Tirta, another bicycle-boy, whispered into his ear.

"Mister what?" asked Pax.

"Just Mister," said Tirta.

"What does he want?" Pax whispered back.

Tirta shrugged. "He asks boys to make deliveries. He will pay double the money Andy pays."

"Double?" said Pax, eyes wide.

Tirta nodded. "And his driver takes us in his car."

A car? Pax had never been in a car. "It must be drugs," said Pax. He knew about drug selling. The punishment for selling drugs was death by hanging.

Tirta shrugged. "Mister said no drugs."

"Do you believe him?" asked Pax.

Tirta shrugged again. "It makes no difference. See, he gives out buzzers. When it beeps and lights up, it means that Mister wants to meet a bicycle-boy." Tirta pulled a little blue-and-silver beeper from his pocket. He pressed a button. It lit up and the beeper beeped.

"You work for Mister too?" Pax asked.

"Sometimes. But he wants more boys," said Tirta.

"Where do you go when the beeper goes off?" asked Pax.

"Do you know the kebab-seller between the dress shop and the metal-seller?" Tirta's whisper was so low that Pax had to lean in to hear.

"Yes," said Pax.

"We meet there. When the beeper goes off, I have to run

fast. Mister gets angry if he waits too long." Tirta slipped the beeper into his front pocket. "I never keep him waiting."

"And he pays you?" asked Pax.

"Big money, and in American!" said Tirta.

Pax whistled. American money, that was good.

Mister pointed to Tirta. The boy smiled and followed Mister down the stairs.

Pax looked back at Andy. He did not look happy, but then the phone rang.

"Pax," Andy bellowed. Pax leapt up and ran towards the office. "Here, go to this address and pick up a package. They will tell you where to deliver it. Hurry." Andy handed Pax a slip of paper. Pax was the only bicycle-boy who could read.

"Andy, about Mister . . . ?" Pax dithered in front of Andy's desk.

"Stay away from him. Go!" Andy snarled but he did not look up.

Pax dashed down the stairs. It was a good address. Maybe he would get a good tip.

Even though Kai stayed with Ol' May, he still had to follow Pax's rules. First, he had to do homework. Teacher gave Kai special homework. It was difficult work, algebra and geometry. Only when the work was done did Pax say that Kai could play outside of the shack. But he was not to go near the big road. "Promise?" Pax would ask Kai, over and over. Kai would nod and say, "I promise."

Ol' May laughed at Pax. "What you think this learning do? Nothing." She waved her big hands about as if swatting flies.

It was hot. The rains had stopped. Pax came home from the bicycle shop and found Ol' May's hut empty.

"Kai?" he called out. He stood outside. The whole area was quiet. Agung, an old man who lived with his daughter, squatted on his haunches outside his shack. He was the only sign of life. "Agung, have you seen Kai?" Pax called out.

The old man cupped his hand around his ear.

"I said, HAVE YOU SEEN KAI, THE BOY?" Pax shouted.

The man batted the air with a crippled hand and hollered, "Gone to the execution."

"What execution?" Pax asked, but he did not wait for an answer.

Pax ran down the lanes, dodged small carts, leapt over ditches, and smacked back dozens of hanging wires that brought television and electricity to their area. Crates and stacks of filthy dishes lined the alleys. He heard the groan of a machine, the sharp grind of metal scraping against metal. Laundry flapped overhead. He kept running. He turned a corner. And then there they were—a surge of people coming towards him, all smiles. Children led the way, leaping and jumping as if returning from a day in the park.

"Pax, Pax!" Kai cried out, both hands waving in the air. He raced towards him and fell into Pax's arms. Instantly Pax's T-shirt was wet with Kai's tears.

"What has happened?"

"The man's feet kept dancing. They hanged him from a

big thing." Kai turned to Ol' May, who was not far behind. "What was he hanged from?" Kai called out.

"A crane," hollered Ol' May. She was flushed pink from heaving her great bulk around.

"They tied his hands behind his back and put a blindfold over his eyes and then the crane lifted him high in the air." said Kai as he buried his face in Pax's shoulder.

"You are all right," Pax whispered into Kai's ear. Then he turned to Ol' May. "You should not have taken him to see such a thing," he yelled. His voice rose above the noise of the crowd.

"Boy having fun. Dead man a drug dealer, murderer maybe. He deserved to die," jeered Ol' May.

Pax faced Ol' May square. "Kai is just a boy!" he screamed at the woman.

"And you like old man. You no his father. Where you get ideas? I tell you, from foreign woman, Bell. Mad as they come. Killed herself, too. Ha!" Ol' May threw her great paws up in the air.

"She was sick! Don't you talk about her ever again." Pax could have hit Ol' May. He could have shoved her back into the ditch, stepped on her face, and drowned her in the mud. Instead he took Kai's hand and marched down the path towards the shed.

Bell—he was beginning to forgive her.

A man, a stranger, paced outside Ol' May's hut. Pax slowed down. The man was neither young nor old but some age in between. His clothes looked expensive—new and clean. He wore shiny shoes with pointy toes.

"Stay close." Pax pushed Kai behind him. Maybe he was from the city. Maybe he had come to take Kai away. "Who is that?" Pax whispered to Agung, who still squatted on the edge of the road with his knees up against his ears.

"That be Ol' May's son." The old man chuckled.

Pax stopped and stared. Ol' May had a son?

Ol' May's voice rang out in greeting. She pushed past Pax and stumbled towards her son. Her arms were outstretched, her face cracked open into a wide smile. Ol' May son's face contorted in disgust. He turned his back on her and walked into the hut. Ol' May followed. There was a spring in her step.

Pax and Kai waited on the road beside old Agung. They heard shouting and then sobs. The son charged out of the hut as if he were on fire.

"It's always the same." Old Agung chuckled.

"What is?" asked Pax.

"The son hates the mother. He gives her a few coins so that she does not come to the great city and embarrass him. I think he is tired of giving her even a small portion of his money. What use is she to him?" Agung shrugged.

"Stay here," Pax whispered to Kai.

Slowly, silently, Pax walked over to Ol' May's hut and stood on the threshold. There she was, sitting on the floor, her massive head cupped by her gigantic hands. Great mounds of flesh escaped her soiled blouse as her body heaved in sobs. He tried not to recoil from the stench. The shack stank of tobacco, sweat, and stale beer. Coins lay on the bare floor in front of her.

"Ol' May, can I help?" asked Pax. He crouched on his knees in front of her. He felt sorry for her. It wasn't her fault she had the giant disease.

"Get away. Get away!" she screamed. "You are dirty boy. You bring bad luck."

Chapter 13

The bicycle shop closed down. No one knew why. There was just a piece of paper tacked to the door that read "Closed For Good."

Pax cleaned inside railway cars at night and wiped car windows for change during the day. Dodging trucks and cars for a few coins was hard work. Sometimes drivers tried to run him over for fun. Pax needed a better way to make money. All he thought about, day and night, was how to get Kai into a good school.

Teacher said that there was a school that offered scholarships, a real school in a big building with many teachers. Teacher said that there were many good schools in their country. Maybe Kai could sit an exam?

"Does it cost money to write the exam?" asked Pax.

"Yes, but if he gets in, he still must pay more for his uniform and supplies."

Bell's old money box still had five hundred American

dollars in it. Was that a lot of money or not so much? He jingled a few coins in his pocket. He bought rice and vegetables that night but no meat.

Pax put the container of food down on a mat in Ol' May's hut and the three of them scooped out the rice with their fingers.

"You good boy," Ol' May said. Neither had said anything about her son, or about how Ol' May had called Pax a dirty boy. Anyway, that was weeks ago.

Ol' May looked at Kai and said, "See, Pax, Kai looks at you like dog with big soppy eyes." Her laugh sounded like wood burning under a pot, all crackles and pops.

Pax shook his head. "Kai is not a dog," he muttered.

"Yes he is. Look at how he follows you. It's a wonder he does not sniff your behind." This time her laugh knocked her backwards. She rocked on her great ass.

"He is not a dog," Pax repeated, his voice rising.

"Ruff, ruff, a little brown nose sniffing at your bum bum," howled Ol' May as she righted herself.

Kai looked at Pax and held his breath. He waved his palm as if to say, *No, no, Pax. Don't get mad. Please, please.*

"KAI IS NOT A DOG," Pax yelled.

"Ruff, ruff!" She brushed away great globs of tears that rolled down the folds of her face.

"Stop it!" Pax lurched forward and slapped her across her cheek. It was the sound of a dry stick cracking over a knee. His hand left a long red streak. The shock on her face lasted only a moment.

"Pax, no," cried Kai.

Ol' May heaved herself up with a great fart, pulled back her banana-leaf-sized hand, and landed it on Pax's head. He flew back and slammed into the wall of the hut. Ol' May's hut was built with old tires. The mud that held the tires in place cracked.

"Pax!" Kai screamed.

The wall gave way and Pax landed outside in the ditch. Kai's eyes were round. His jaw hung open. How could a boy fly through a wall? He was astonished.

Ol' May looked out through the hole and laughed so hard piss ran down her leg.

Pax stood and shook like a dog. Filthy water dripped from his clothes. His eye began to swell. Kai's head swung back and forth to Ol' May, Pax, Ol' May. He tried to speak but just stared.

"Fix that wall or I will kill you next time," Ol' May bellowed.

The next evening Pax started back to Ol' May's hut at sunset. He had washed many shop windows and had a few coins in his pocket. He was tired, bone-tired. His eyelids drooped as he shuffled down the path. Tonight he would not go to the train station to clean.

Kai ran down a lane towards him. The algebra book and encyclopedia were clutched to his chest.

"What are you doing here? Why are you carrying those?" Pax pointed to the books.

"Ol' May is gone," said Kai.

"Gone! Where would she go?" asked Pax.

Kai shrugged. "I was playing and she came out of the house with a big bag and her mat and then she ran down the road."

Pax thought for a moment. Ol' May could not run anywhere. Her thighs would bang against each other; her lungs would burst. And then he knew. Knowledge was fuel. Pax sprinted down the lane. His legs carried him forward with the force of a lion after prey.

"Pax, wait. WAIT!" Kai called after him.

The books were heavy. Kai could not keep up, but Pax could not stop. His heart hammered in his chest, sweat flew off of him, his arms pumped, propelling him faster and faster. "No, no, no," he muttered through clenched teeth. He rounded corners, leapt over baskets and crates. He broke through a line of laundry and got caught in an electrical cord that hung too low. He slashed at it as if his hands were knives. Merchants cried out; people yelled. He didn't stop until he came to Ol' May's broken-down hut.

Pax leapt up the steps and lurched into the room. There was nothing, not a pot, not a bowl. He flung back a thin curtain.

Her piss-pot was full. It was a stinking, filthy brew. He kicked it over with his foot. The liquid splashed across the small space and up the walls. He pulled up the floorboard. Gone. Empty. Ol' May had found the money box. She had stolen it. She had taken their future.

That night Pax lay in the dark in Ol' May's hut. But he was angry, angrier than he had ever been. Angrier than when Bell had died and betrayed him. They had nothing now.

As the moon rose Pax got up, sat outside Ol' May's hut, and looked at the hole in the ground where the Pink House had once stood. That life was gone, as if it had never been. Pax looked up at the night sky and thought of praying. Teacher's words floated back. "If you need anything, pray to God and He will help you," he had said.

"God? God, are you there? Can you hear me?"

The stars looked like little holes in the sky. If he pressed his eye against one, could he see the other world? Could he see heaven?

"God, can you see us?" he whispered. His words drifted away.

Praying did not help. He clenched his hands into tight balls. He would just have to work twice as hard. He thought of Mister and his car. But what if Mister was a drug dealer? What if Pax was caught with drugs? He would be hanged, and what would happen to Kai then?

Over the next weeks Pax got a job pushing a wheelbarrow filled with vegetables through the streets. He hauled crates on his back, trapped rats, and carried water.

At night, as Kai slept on the floor of Ol' May's hut, Pax counted the coins. He made barely enough to feed the two of them, but Kai still went to school for three hours a day. There was no one to take care of Kai after school and so Pax worried.

Kai was given more rules. He must return from school and stay inside the hut. "You must listen to me. Boys left on their own, without family, might be stolen. Boys disappear," said Pax. He thought that his words might scare Kai, but they didn't. Kai knew that, no matter what, Pax would keep him safe.

One day, like every day, Pax returned from work exhausted and bone-weary. He carried a half loaf of bread. That was all he could afford. They had not eaten meat in weeks. He saw Kai standing on the road in front of Ol' May's hut. Kai's face was stained with tears.

"Tell me?" Pax kneeled down in front of him. Kai shook his head.

At that moment two men came out of Ol' May's hut and stood on the wooden steps. "This place belongs to us now." The tallest man stepped forward. He threw the algebra book and encyclopedia onto the path. "Take them and go."

Exhaustion disappeared. Again. "We live here. This is our place," Pax yelled, his voice quavering with fury. The bread slipped out of his hand and fell into the dirt.

"No, Pax," Kai cried. He stood between the man and Pax, put his hands on Pax's stomach, and pushed.

The man jumped away from the hut, pulled back his leg, and kicked Kai in the back. Kai fell into Pax's arms. Rage surged through Pax.

"Get out of the way," Pax muttered as he pushed Kai behind him. "This is our house." Pax lowered his head like a little bull and charged at the man. He hit the man in the chest. Shocked, winded, he fell back, his arms fanning the air. Pax had never boxed before but his hands seemed to know what to do. He clenched his fists and lunged towards the smaller man. The smaller man pulled out a gun and smiled.

"Pax!" Kai screamed.

Pax reached for Kai.

"Please, Pax." Tears circled Kai's eyes.

Pax stood still, suspended. Kai picked up the bread and handed it to Pax. Heads high, the two walked down the path towards the street.

Chapter 14

There were hundreds of street children, some lying beside the train tracks, some in back alleys, most on the pavements beside roads.

Kai slept on a piece of cardboard. His head rested on the encyclopedia. Pax lay beside him on the cement sidewalk. Algebra was his pillow. They woke up stiff and tired, as if they had never been to sleep.

Kai no longer went to the local school. There was a new teacher now. He did not care that Kai was very smart. He demanded money, school supplies, and a new uniform. Kai's uniform had been left in Ol' May's hut, and anyway, he had outgrown it.

During the day Pax cleaned car windows and Kai stood nearby. He wanted to work too. Why shouldn't he? All the other kids his age were working. Pax could hear Bell's words, "First they beg, and not long after that, they sell. And do you know what they sell? Themselves!" That would never happen to Kai, never. But slowly Pax was worn down.

Money was food. Kai begged. But when the streets emptied and he had collected enough coins to buy fruit and bread, Kai sat and opened the encyclopedia to letter Q. Quantum mechanics.

"Pax, do you know what photons are?" he yelled across the traffic.

"Tell me," Pax yelled back, although he did not listen to the answer.

"It says that quantum mechanics shows that light and all other forms of electromagnetic radiation come in units called *photons.*"

Pax nodded and kept on polishing car windows. And then a miracle. An arm reached out of a car window and handed him one American dollar. Pax looked at the money in his hand. Cars, trucks, donkey carts all threatened to mow him down, but Pax did not notice. One dollar!

Pax looked over at Kai, who sat cross-legged on the pavement, his head buried in the book. His feet were as black as tarpaper and scabby as tree bark. Pax's flip-flops would do a while longer, but Kai needed shoes.

They headed to the laneway of shops and stalls, each one carved into the wall, each with a man or woman sitting guard over their secondhand goods. Kai lagged behind as Pax poked through a dozen stalls.

"What about this?" Kai held up a Batman T-shirt.

"A shirt is not a shoe!" said Pax.

Shoes came in tall barrels. Pax sifted through old sandals, running shoes, worn boots—any type of shoe that might fit a seven-year-old. Kai gave up and sat on the pavement, his back against a wall, the book between his legs and his chest, his knees up around his ears. Shopping was boring.

"Aha!" cried Pax, like a miner striking gold. He held up the perfect pair of shoes. They were brown with blue rubber soles. They might have been white once but color did not matter. They were the right size and they had LACES!

"How much?" Pax dangled the runners from his fingertips.

A woman wrapped in a shawl held up two crooked fingers. "Two American dollars," she said.

"One American dollar." Pax waved the green bill in the air.

She leaned forward and snatched it out of his hand.

Pax held the books as Kai slipped the runners on his feet. "This is how you tie shoelaces," said Pax as he tied the laces tight. Grinning, Kai walked up and down the pavement, hands outstretched as if he were walking a tightrope. He wrapped his arms around Pax and buried his face in his belly.

"Do you know what's best about them?" Kai looked up, his face pink with happiness. Pax shook his head. "They are the perfect temperature inside."

For the first time in a long time, Pax laughed.

That night, Kai slept with his shoes on his feet, tied up tight. Pax lay on a piece of cardboard beside him. When they awoke, the shoes were gone.

Chapter 15

Days and nights came and went. Saturdays were no different from Mondays since every day they had to eat. Sometimes they were given free food handed to them through a little window in a square, blue truck. Often the cooks inside the truck reached out and hit the children with their spoons. "Don't be greedy," they said.

One morning, as the sky was lightening, Pax and Kai stumbled towards the food truck. Kai rubbed his eyes with balled-up fists. He was still sleepy. Already there was a line of street children waiting, some with bowls in their hands, others with paper shaped into cones. The truck was late. Pax held the encyclopedia under his arm, and Kai clutched the algebra book to his chest.

Living on the street had changed Pax. Despite being constantly tired, despite feeling as if his bones were rubbery and his insides were crawling with ants, his ears perked at the smallest noise. His eyes darted from side to side. His nose twitched. It was hard to remember simple things, like how to multiply two numbers, but he could sense danger as if it had a sound or a smell.

That morning, in the blue, predawn light, he spied a car waiting near the spot where the food truck was usually parked. He looked closer. It was an unmarked police car, he was sure of it. And inside were two policemen out of uniform. They were pretending to be sleeping. Pax's shoulders went up as he backed away.

"Kai, stay close," he hissed. The other children milling about looked like shadows and moved like ghosts in the early light.

"Pax, what's wrong?" Kai whispered.

"Nothing." He was lying. Pax grabbed Kai's hand and turned to run away.

They heard footsteps—*clomp-clomp*—the sound that boots made. It happened in an instant. They came from behind. The police were dressed in black and wore plastic face-shields. *Clomp-clomp*. They circled the children. The children began to dart in all directions. There was screaming and panic as one child, then another, tried to break free.

"Hold tight," Pax cried out.

A police truck pulled up to the curb. The back doors opened. Two, then three boys were tossed inside like sacks of rice. A policeman planted a gloved hand on Pax's shoulder. It was as if the claw of a great flying beast had him pinned.

"Where are you taking us?" Pax cried out.

The answers were grunts and rumbles. In a surge of strength Pax pulled away from the policeman's grip.

The voice of a street boy rose up above the clamor. "They are taking us to prison," he cried.

Prison? Pax weaved and dodged but held Kai's hand firmly.

The police waved their sticks. They formed a line. A policeman spoke through a megaphone. "A new apartment building will be built here. Come with us and we will take you to a safe place."

Pax looked every which way, his head turning as if on a spit. He was panting. Another policeman raised his stick to a small girl. She was screaming. This was their chance.

"Drop the book," cried Pax.

Kai held his algebra book closer to his chest. Pax dropped the encyclopedia and knocked the algebra book out of Kai's hand. Kai cried out.

"Hold on." Pax lowered his head like a bull about to charge and lunged through the police line. "Run, Kai," he cried.

A policeman's stick came down on the side of his head. Dazed, Pax put his hand to his head. Blood poured through his fingers. He dropped to his knees. Groaning, eyes closed, he rolled onto his side.

Kai flung himself over Pax's body. *Whomp, whomp, whomp*—the policeman's stick sliced the air and cut through Kai's thin shirt. Kai cried out.

"Leave him alone." Pax lifted his bloody head from the pavement. He rested on his hands. One knee went up and then the other. He rose up like a monster from the deep, raised his arms in the air, and roared. His face was contorted in rage. "Get back, Kai," Pax screamed. Kai scrambled away.

Pax was as big as a house, as fierce as any animal in the forest. The policeman cowered. Pax lashed out and grabbed the policeman's stick. The policeman stumbled and toppled backwards onto the ground. Pax could not be stopped. He raised the stick over his head.

"Pax, no!" Kai screamed. More policemen were coming towards them. Kai grabbed the back of Pax's shirt and pulled. The policeman on the ground was now up on his knees. "Please, Pax!" Kai shouted. There were screams and now smoke.

Pax stopped and sniffed. Tear gas? He dropped the policeman's stick and grabbed Kai's hand. They ran like one person. The shouting increased. Sirens. They ducked behind a car, stopped, then ran again.

"There." Pax pointed to an alley. He gave Kai a push, waited until Kai was at the entrance to the alley, then followed. No one knew the paths and alleys better than Pax.

"Hide." Pax pushed Kai inside a tiny shack made of corrugated tin and strips of tarpaper. It was no taller than Pax and no wider than the span of his arms. "Are you hurt?" asked Pax. Rays of morning sun shone through the slats. Pax lifted Kai's shirt. The welts on Kai's back were thin, red lines but there was no blood, no open wounds.

Kai shook his head. "It doesn't hurt." It was Kai's turn to lie.

Pax held him close. "It will be all right. Close your eyes," he whispered.

"But it is not nighttime," said Kai. His lips fluttered, his eyes filled with tears. He was trying very hard not to cry.

"We must stay out of sight." Pax was careful not to touch Kai's back. He reached up and touched the side of his own head. The blood had stopped, but his ear was ringing.

Pax looked up at the tin that formed a partial roof over the shed. He could see slivers of sky, birds. He wanted to see past the sky to something beyond, something that might help them.

"Help us, Bell."

He spoke as if his thoughts could be carried up to her spirit, as if she were still there, watching over them, protecting them as she always had. She had said that every bad day has an ending and every good day a beginning. But what if that wasn't true? What if a bad day followed a bad day? What if it was a step down, then another step down, then another and another? What if there was no way back? How could he turn around on the steps and go back up?

"Pax, tell me a story," whispered Kai.

"Not now, someone might hear." Outside a baby cried, dogs barked, peddlers cried out, and in the far distance traffic droned. The sounds of horns and sirens were muted.

No one noticed or cared about two boys hiding in a shed.

"Please," Kai begged.

Pax took a deep breath. "Once there was a king and queen and they had a baby named Kai." Pax paused. He thought of Bell and of the facility she had chosen for Kai.

"Why are you stopping?" Kai whispered.

"I am thinking."

"What are you thinking?"

"I am thinking that I have another story to tell you," said Pax.

"Is it about me?" Kai asked.

"Of course. Let me think."

The two were quiet for a few moments.

"I am ready," said Pax. "Once there was a boy named Kai. He was made of dust and air and yet he was strong. He was handsome and smart, the smartest boy around." Pax wiped his face with his hand.

"Was he the smartest boy in the kingdom?" asked Kai.

"Yes, but he did not live in a kingdom," said Pax.

"Was he a prince?" Kai sat up.

"He was just like a prince. His beauty was prince-like but he had no princely clothes, no castle, no white horse with flaring nostrils or a golden saddle to carry him to great dinners and grand balls. He did not have parents called King and Queen. He had no parents at all."

The descriptions came easily. The more effort Pax put into the story, the better he felt. His heart stopped beating so fast and thoughts came quickly.

"Then how could he be a prince?" asked Kai.

"Because in his heart . . . hush!" Footsteps thumped down the path mere inches from their hiding place. The two froze in place. Breath caught in their throats.

"Pax?" Kai whispered.

Pax shook his head. *Wait.* He mouthed the word. The sounds outside the shed receded and so Pax continued. "The boy was so smart that everyone decided that he would be a prince."

"Who is everyone?"

"All the people who lived in the kingdom."

"But you said—"

"Do you want me to tell the story?"

"Yes." Kai clamped his mouth shut.

Pax continued. "This boy lived in the slums and grew like a tree among the open sewers, the dirt, and the garbage. One day a man came along and said to the boy, 'If you are to grow up and be a real prince, you must leave all the people you know and come with me to a special school.'"

"What was the man's name?" asked Kai.

"Peter," said Pax.

"We know a Peter."

"Don't interrupt. The young boy did not want to leave his . . . people . . ."

"What people?"

"Never mind."

"What was the name of the prince-school?" asked Kai.

Pax did not hesitate. "Oxford. That's where they teach boys how to be prince-like."

"Is it a princess-school too?"

"No. Yes. Maybe, I don't know. Stop interrupting. The boy did not want to go with Peter, but then he realized that if he was going to fulfill his destiny—"

"I know what destiny is," Kai stated.

"What is it?"

"Fate. Bell said so."

"When did she say that?" asked Pax.

"A long time ago. I remember." Kai was pleased with himself.

"You remember everything," said Pax. He looked down at

Kai. He could feel a tickle at the back of his throat and a sting behind his eyes. He should have listened to Bell. They could not live on the streets. Sooner or later one of them would get sick, attacked, or hurt. Kai should be in school, a real school. He had been wrong to take Kai away from that life, wrong to think he could protect him.

"Pax, if it is a princess-school too, then maybe the prince could meet a princess and they could live happily ever after," said Kai.

Pax let out a muffled sob.

"Pax, are you crying?" Kai reached up and touched Pax's face.

"No."

"Your face is wet."

"Close your eyes. Rest," said Pax.

"I didn't like that story. I only like the last part."

"Close your eyes."

They hid in the shed for the entire day. The sun was setting when they emerged. They were stiff and walked like two crippled old men. They went to a public water tap at the edge of the road. The government had put it in, but the water that came out of the spout was brown and it made people who drank it sick. Still, they washed away layers of dust and flakes of dried blood.

"Come, we have a long walk ahead of us," said Pax.

"Where are we going?" Kai asked.

"To the city," said Pax.

"We live in the city."

"We are going to where the big buildings are."

"But it's dark." Kai looked up at the night sky.

"No one will see us. We will be there by the time the sun is up."

Chapter 16

They walked. They hung off the back of a truck for a while, then walked again. The road underfoot was smooth. People dressed differently in this part of the city. There were many cars. They begged along the way.

Rich people were not very generous, but after several hours of begging, they had enough money to buy a mango from a fruit-seller. It was old and bruised. Pax split it open. They ate the juicy flesh. Kai sucked on the pit. Pax used the mango skin to cool the sores on Kai's back. It was sticky.

The glass buildings were no longer gleaming castles in the distance. They were now close enough to touch.

"Smell," said Pax.

Kai sniffed. The air smelled different—fresher. The ground was clean and there were no ditches. There were cemented spaces everywhere and spots of green, too, like rugs. They knew this was grass, but not once had they ever stepped on such a thing. There were fewer donkeys and carts, fewer bike-taxis and scooters.

"Does the queen live here?" asked Kai.

"No." Pax shook his head.

"Where are we going?" asked Kai for the hundredth time.

"To a *facility*," said Pax.

Kai stopped asking questions. He was out of breath.

The roads were bigger, the traffic faster. They did what others did: stopped at lights, crossed when the light turned green. There were statues in store windows.

Kai pointed up. "What does it say?"

"Gucci," said Pax, although he pronounced it *Goose-seee*. Tall trees were growing out of giant concrete containers. The walkways were broad, big enough for cars.

Kai looked into a tall barrel. "Look!" He pulled out a half-eaten sandwich. He was about to bite into it when a woman grabbed it from him, tossed it back into the bin, and handed him money.

"That's garbage. Go buy yourself lunch," she said.

Kai reached out to touch her, to say thank you. Horrified, the woman pulled back and spun away. Kai handed Pax the money.

The two looked up and down the street. There were no street vendors, no kebab-sellers hovering over coals. Where would someone buy food if there were no carts selling food? Kai peered back into the garbage bin. His sandwich was now way at the bottom.

"Look!" Kai pointed to pictures of hamburgers and kebabs on a sign. Under the sign was the word *"Delicious."* The two pressed their noses against a window. There were people eating inside. "Do we have enough money?" asked Kai.

Pax nodded, but he wasn't too sure. He opened the glass door.

A man in a brown-and-white uniform came running over. His nose crinkled up. "You can't come in here." He pushed them back out on the street.

"But we have money." Pax held up the bills.

"You have to have a bath before you come in here. You stink." The man plucked the bills out of Pax's hand. "Tell me what you want and I will bring it out to you." They did not know what to say.

The man returned with a bottle of water and two meat sandwiches and long potatoes. "Hamburgers and fries," said the man. He did not give back change.

Pax and Kai squatted on their haunches, ate, then licked the paper the hamburgers came in. There were no gritty bits in the water they drank, nothing that stuck in the teeth. It went straight down the throat and made their insides feel clean.

"It's . . ." Kai hunted around for a word to describe the taste of water.

"It's *deeee-licious*," said Pax. They both laughed, but despite a full belly Pax felt empty inside, hollow. Soon they would find Peter.

Pax stared up at the buildings that surrounded them. Which one was a *facility* for children? There were no children anywhere. They put the hamburger wrappings in the bin and walked up the steps of the first building. They stood in front of the revolving doors.

"What do we do?" asked Kai.

"Watch."

People approached the revolving doors with one hand stretched out. They walked inside and came out the other side, which was actually now inside. But if they didn't jump inside, then they would end up outside and have to start all over again.

"Ready?" asked Pax. Kai nodded. "One, two three . . ." They leapt.

Kai screamed. His foot was caught in the revolving door.

"STOP! STOP!" Pax banged on the glass. "HELP!"

A security guard came running. All sorts of people gathered around. Two men stopped the door from revolving. Pax, stuck behind glass, could only watch. Kai was pulled away from the revolving door. Pax spun around not once but twice before he could escape. Breathing hard, he bent down beside Kai. "Are you okay?" Sobbing, Kai nodded.

"What are you two doing here? What do you want?" the guard yelled.

"I don't think that shouting at them will help the situation." A man in a suit spoke to the guard.

Pax looked up. The man had a soft, dark face, lined like wrinkled cloth. His eyes were watery and brown.

"What is it you want, boys?" He leaned down and spoke gently.

"We are trying to find *the facility*, the place for children to go to school," said Pax, bravely.

"You are in the business area. I think you want the government buildings. Come. Can you stand?" he asked Kai.

Blinking back tears, Kai stood. The man felt Kai's ankle. "Nothing broken. I expect you have had a shock. Go down this road for two blocks and turn to your left. Do you know your left?"

Kai raised his left hand, proudly. Pax scowled. Of course they knew their left hand from their right hand.

"Excellent. You will see a white building. That is Children's Services. Go inside and you will see a big desk with a man or woman sitting behind it. Ask for help there." The man smiled. The guard grumbled.

"Thank you," said Pax.

"See that sign over there? It is a washroom. You can go and wash up if you want," said the man.

The guard stepped forward. "Sir . . . I don't think . . ."

The man reached into his pocket and handed the guard some bills. "Pass this along to the cleaners." The man gave the guard a hard look.

"Yes Mr. Golzar." The guard tipped his hat.

Pax and Kai pushed open the washroom door. "What is this place?" Pax whispered.

The lighting was dim. A long silver trough reached from one end of the room to the other. A giant mirror was above it. Pax reached out and waved his hand. Water spouted out of a long pipe! He leapt back as Kai let out a tiny yelp.

"What is it?" Kai asked.

Pax shook his head. It was like a long, sideways shower. "Do people lie in it?" Above the long, silver sink-like thing were little silver buttons.

"Push the button," said Kai.

Pax took a deep breath and pushed. Out came white syrup. He sniffed. "Soap!" It wasn't like Bell's soap; it wasn't yellow and hard, it was white and foamy. "Climb up," he told Kai.

Kai peeled off his brown shorts and yellow T-shirt and lay down in the trough. His hands were pressed to his sides. He might have been in a very, very narrow coffin. Pax pushed the buttons, all of them. Kai giggled. The water was warm. They took turns washing themselves in the trough.

Naked and wet, the two stood beside the long sink. How to get dry?

"What are those?" Kai pointed to silver boxes on the walls. Pax pushed the button on one box. Out came blasts of warm air. Kai squealed with delight.

"Put your head under," said Pax.

In the end, their hair stood straight up in clumps. They looked in the mirror and laughed themselves silly. They had eaten. They were clean. Almost clean. Their clothes were still dirty.

"Look, Pax." Both boys looked at the mess they had created. Water was everywhere. Bell would have been furious.

Kai pointed to a stack of white paper. The paper was better than either had ever seen before. To use it like rags seemed wrong, but what choice did they have? Within minutes the place was shining, and not a speck of water was on the counter or floor.

"Pax, I need to go pee," said Kai.

Pax looked around. There was a wall of silver doors but no toilet. "Wait, we will be outside soon."

The two left the washroom. A woman stood outside with a giant bucket on wheels, a mop, and all sorts of bottles and jugs. As the boys walked past her, she gave them a pained look, then she barged into the washroom. A moment later she was back out, standing by the washroom door, her mouth agape. She looked at the guard and mouthed the words, "It's clean!"

Pax and Kai walked across the cold marble floor. They stopped at the revolving door.

"Over here." The guard held open a side door.

They ran down the steps, raced around to the side of the building, and peed against the wall.

"What does it say?" asked Kai. He could read well enough but the gold plaque on the wall was too high.

"It says Children's Services."

Pax paused. They would take Kai away. He would go to a special school, write tests, and eventually go to university. Oxford University—the school for princes-in-training.

"Pax, what's wrong?" asked Kai.

"Nothing, come on." They walked into another great building. There was not a child in sight.

"Please, we would like to see Peter." Pax spoke to the woman behind a desk.

"Peter who?" she snapped. She was not very old, but her glasses made her look fierce, like a cat.

"Dr. Peter Bennett. We are from the Pink House, except it is gone now. It was run by Bell, but she is gone now too.

Peter came and tested Kai. This is Kai. Kai is very smart. We are supposed to go into a facility. We would like to go there now, please." Pax took a deep breath.

"Mrs. Jacour, would you please come to reception," the woman said, speaking into a telephone. "Here," she reached into a drawer and pulled out two candies wrapped in crinkly paper. "Sit over there and wait." She handed them the candies. "Thank-you," said Pax and Kai. It was a nice thing to do, but why was she so grumpy?

There were big chairs by the window, but instead the woman pointed to two stools near the door. They sat. They sat for a very long time. Finally another woman appeared.

"There." The woman behind the desk motioned towards Pax and Kai.

The second woman, much older than the one at the desk, walked over to them. Bell had taught them to stand when a lady came into the room. This wasn't exactly a room but they stood anyway.

"My name is Mrs. Jacour. What do you two want?" she asked. If she was impressed by their good manners, she did not let on.

"We are from—" Pax was about to start again but the woman put up her hand.

"If you are going to tell me that you are from the Pink House, I will stop you right there. We have all the children from that ridiculous orphanage in our care."

"You don't have us," said Kai, in all innocence.

"I can assure you all the children from that place are accounted for. Now, where do you live?"

"He needs to go to school." Pax poked Kai in the back. Reluctantly Kai stepped forward.

"I need your names," said the woman. She was starting to sound very cross.

"Please, can we see Peter?" Pax was beginning to panic.

"Peter who? There is no Peter here."

"Dr. Bennett. Please," Pax said.

She frowned. "You two wait right here." Then she turned and left. Was she going to get a security guard? The police? Her heels *click-clacked* across a floor made of shiny stone.

"What do we do now?" Kai looked up at Pax.

He swallowed hard. "We go back."

For the second night in a row, they walked.

Chapter 17

Pax returned to washing windows, cleaning trains, pushing wheelbarrows, and polishing shoes at the train station. He made enough money to keep them fed. Finding a place to sleep was the hardest part.

"Who said you could stand here?" The boy hovering over Pax and Kai was the leader of the pack. He was bigger than the boys who stood behind him. His mouth curled over his teeth and he had black marks on his hands—drawings made with ink.

Kai moved closer to Pax and leaned against him. Kai's eyelids slipped down. Dark black circles hung beneath each eye, and his cheeks were hollow. They needed a place to sleep—any place. A piece of sidewalk would do.

"We're not doing anything," said Pax. They had moved three times in the last three days. No matter where they went, there were bands of boys threatening them.

"You are taking up our air." The leader spat out the words like bullets. The boys behind him laughed.

"We want to join you," said Pax.

"Do you have any money?" asked the head boy. Pax shook his head.

"Then what good are you to us?" The boys jeered. They jumped around. Their movements were jittery.

Drugs, thought Pax. He was beginning to understand the street.

"We can read," mumbled Kai.

"Read! Read what? Maybe you could read us a stoooooooory," a boy with sores on his face piped up.

The leader looked at Kai. Pax could see him thinking. His eyes grew narrow. He picked his teeth with a small knife. "You can stay for a few days and then we will see. Call me Rambo." He smiled. It wasn't a nice smile.

Rambo was old, maybe sixteen. Rambo was the boss of their street family. He wore a scarf on his head. Rambo carried a small knife and a gun. "It's American. In America every child gets a gun." Rambo petted his gun like it was a small animal.

Pax let them think that he and Kai were brothers. It was easier that way.

"You work?" Rambo asked Pax.

Pax nodded.

"You give me half of what you earn," said Rambo.

"Half?" Pax shook his head.

"Half or go on your way. Leave the boy with me." He pointed to Kai.

Pax considered. So far he'd been able to take Kai with him to his jobs. He helped with cleaning and sometimes he made a few coins by begging. But the shoeshine boss did not want little kids hanging around. "Tourists come and complain if they see little kids working. Ha! They would prefer that the kids starve—but out of sight," said the boss. It was a good job, although paying for the polish cost him half a day's wage. Half was better than nothing, but now he would have to give half of that to Rambo.

"He is only seven," said Pax.

All the boys laughed, and Rambo said, "I have been living on my own since I was four."

One of the other boys shoved him. "Four, you can't count that high." They laughed all over again. Rambo didn't laugh.

"I could teach you to count," said Kai. The boys stopped laughing.

"I could teach you a thing or two, too." Rambo took a drag on his rolled cigarette.

"He didn't mean anything," said Pax. He bent down and whispered into Kai's ear, "Just be good and stay out of their way. Don't wander anywhere. I will be back as fast as I can. Soon I will have the money for you to go back to school. I will make many tips. Just stay here, promise?"

Kai nodded. He looked over at the gang of boys. Most wore hats; all wore jackets with signs on them. They turned their backs on Pax and Kai.

The two fell asleep around a metal drum that spat sparks.

Pax would shine shoes for twelve hours. All day he'd be hunched over, his arms moving back and forth. The tips were good. But his boss would come along and inspect his work. He'd put out his hand, then rub his fingers together. After taking half of his money, the boss searched Pax's pockets, and when he found nothing, he went through the shoeshine kit.

"Don't think you can cheat me. I know all your tricks," he said.

What tricks? Pax shook his head.

Once, when he had packed up and was ready to leave, the boss said, "Wait, I have another job for you." He handed Pax a rag and pointed to his car. He did not pay Pax for his work.

Pax saw many things on the street. And he knew he had to find a regular job and get Kai away from all this. He thought of Mister and the boy Tirta. Once or twice he thought he'd spotted Tirta on the streets. If only he knew what it was Mister was up to.

As the sun set, Pax headed back to the street he now lived on. He would get Kai and together they would eat rice from a food truck. He took the shortcut.

"Where is Kai?" he asked the boy with the sores on his face.

"You are late. Your little brother wanted to make money, to work. Rambo took him for a walk," said one with an eagle blazed on his shirt.

Pax leapt at the guy, grabbed him by the throat, and cried out, "Where are they?"

"Hey, watch it. The kid wants to work." The boy batted Pax in the ear.

Pax stumbled. "What kind of work?" He was screaming. He shoved the boy, full force, two hands on his chest. "I said, where are they?" Pax swung his arm and landed a fist in the boy's stomach.

The boy bent over, groaning. "On the street, maybe."

Pax ran. The street was long. They could be anywhere.

Pax raced out to the main road. There were cars, trucks, mules pulling wagons, and bike-taxis, and pushcarts, and all manner of things with wheels. People yelled at each other, shook their fists, thumbed their noses, and barged across the busy road. He ran. He ran.

Think, think. Where would Rambo take him? To a main intersection.

He dodged traffic and ran again. He spotted them. Rambo and Kai were on the opposite side of the street. Pax yelled out. His voice was lost in the traffic noise. He called out again, and again. There was no place to cross.

Rambo had his head in a car window. He was talking to the driver. Kai was standing on the pavement. He was rubbing his eyes. The man shook his head. Rambo motioned with his hands. What was he doing? They were haggling! There was traffic, six lanes of it.

"KAI!"

Pax ran out onto the road. Cars honked. He dodged, weaved, but got pushed back by a truck. It was a bike that knocked him down. A car stopped. He scrambled up over its hood. There was more yelling.

"Kai, Kai!"

Kai was getting into the car. The car pulled away from the

curb. Rambo was walking away. He had cash in his hand. He licked his fingers and flipped through bills.

Pax dodged one car, then another. He leapt in front of the car that Kai was in, arms wide. Kai was in the backseat. Pax closed his eyes and waited to be hit.

Horns honked, hundreds of them. The brakes squealed. Pax opened his eyes. The car had stopped. Pax stared at the driver, the one who would steal Kai. The driver was not young, not old. Mustache. Wide-set light eyes, yellow hair.

"Kai, get out! Get out!" Pax screamed.

The car door opened. After that, Pax could remember only snapshots of events, like blinking. Another car coming towards him, the wind knocked out of him. Rolling over the hood. Pain. Running. Holding Kai's hand. Vomiting.

Pax's chest was wrapped in bandages. "You are lucky that your ribs were not broken," said the nurse. Lucky? A medical truck cruised the streets at night giving out bottled water and advice. Sometimes a nurse traveled in the truck. She had wrapped up Pax's chest in a white bandage, and she gave Kai an orange.

"Since you are here, I will give you a shot," she said. The nurse held up a needle, then pushed it into Pax's upper arm. "It's only tetanus. If you get a cut, it will prevent you from getting sick."

Pax nodded. They had had shots before. Bell had insisted.

Pax and Kai left the first-aid truck and set out. It was dark, past midnight. Kai was tired.

"Pax, what are we looking for?" asked Kai.

"Don't talk so loud. I am looking for a boy," said Pax as he looked down at the children sleeping on the street.

"Who?" Kai whispered.

"His name is Tirta," said Pax.

"Who is Tirta?"

"I met him at the bicycle shop."

At night the streets were layered with children. They lay in all directions, some in sleeping bags donated by foreigners, others on sheets of cardboard, most curled up on the pavement using sandals and rubber shoes, or each other, as pillows.

Pax crept along the sidewalk, gazing into face after face. Kai trailed behind. "Tirta?" He shook the shoulder of a boy. The boy snapped to attention, eyes alert, hands up. "Sorry," said Pax. Every child looked the same as the next—all dirty, all unnaturally thin.

Pax held his hand up in the air. Kai stopped. Pax peered down at a sleeping boy. It was him, Tirta.

"Wait here," Pax whispered. He tiptoed around a few others before kneeling down. "Tirta, wake up," Pax murmured into the sleeping boy's ear.

The boy jolted upright, hands clenched and ready to fight.

"It's me, Pax, from the bicycle shop."

Tirta took a breath. "What do you want?" He was more frightened than annoyed.

"To meet Mister," said Pax.

The boy looked around, stood, then motioned Pax to follow him. They stood with their backs against a wall.

"How much?" Tirta held up the beeper.

Pax was confused. "I just want to meet him," he said.

Tirta nodded. Snot ran out of his nose. Pax sat back on his haunches. The snot was red.

"You buy this and tell Mister that I am sick. That I cannot work for him now," said Tirta. He smeared the blood from his nose across his cheek. His eyes were yellow and his skin tinged green.

Pax nodded as he reached into his pocket and handed Tirta a few coins. Tirta snatched them up. He was smaller than Pax remembered, as if he were growing backwards.

"When the buzzer goes off, go to the kebab-seller near the park, between the dress shop and the metal-seller. Remember what I said. I am sick. I will get well soon," said Tirta.

Pax nodded. He reached into his other pocket and gave the boy all the coins he had.

Chapter 18

The buzzer went off after dawn. Pax and Kai now slept in a culvert very near where the Pink House had once stood. It was a round, cement tube—like a tunnel. At first they were shooed away by the people who lived in the huts and shacks, but Pax said, "I lived in the Pink House." Some remembered Bell, one or two recognized Pax, others took pity. They gave them food, but they had their own children to feed.

"Hurry," said Pax.

Kai, still mostly asleep, scrambled up. There were no mats to roll, no clothes to put on, no tongue-scrapers or bars of soap to use. They owned nothing. Kai tried to keep up with Pax, who walked with his head forward as if pushing against a wind.

"Look!" Pax came to an abrupt stop and pointed. A long, sleek, white car with black windows was pulled up to the edge of the pavement. A great wave of dusty children swarmed the car and pounded the windshield with rock-hard fists. They screamed for money, candy, an empty water bottle—

anything that dripped from the hands of a rich man had value. The driver leapt out of the car and swished them away, his arms propelled like windmills.

"It's him. It's Mister," said Pax. At last their luck had turned. Pax held up the buzzer.

The back window rolled down and a hand with long, curly fingernails beckoned. "Come, come," said the hand.

Mister's birdlike face appeared behind the curved hand. He gazed at Pax curiously. The long fingernails motioned them forward.

Pax grabbed Kai's hand and whispered as the two ran towards the car, "Thank you, God." And to Kai he said, "Don't talk."

The driver held back the other street children. A path was cleared to the car. The back door opened. "Enter," said the man. And then he said to Pax and Kai, "Sit."

They climbed in. The cool air inside the car took their breath away. Where did it come from? Did this man have the power to control weather? The car had long black seats facing each other. This was not like the other cars either had seen on the roads.

"Where is the other boy?" asked Mister.

"He is not well. I am here to take his place. I used to work for Andy at the bicycle shop, I can read and write, I know all the streets, I can make lots of deliveries, this is my brother, he can read and write too." Pax spoke in one long, breathless sentence.

Mister smiled. He handed them candy wrapped in gold foil. The man called the candy "toffee" and said it was better to suck it slowly than to bite into it.

"You want to work for me?" asked Mister. The nub of toffee swished around in Mister's mouth, popping in and out like a little golden fish in a murky pond.

Pax nodded. Kai looked at Pax and then he bobbed his head too.

Mister took a cloth out of his pocket and covered his nose. *We smell*, thought Pax. He gave them a box. It was small, light, and made of cardboard.

"Do you know the fruit-seller on Argle Road?" the man asked.

"Yes," said Pax, through toffee-teeth.

"There is an alley between the fruit-seller and the taxi stand. Take this box and wait in the alley. Someone will come and say, 'Good boys.' He will give you money to buy two kebabs and then he will take the box."

That was all? Just that? Pax was so excited he felt as if bubbles were coming up his throat.

Chapter 19

The buzzer went off. "It's him! It's Mister. Kai, wake up. It will be a good day." Pax gave him a nudge. *"Every bad day has an ending. Every good day has a beginning."* Bell's words.

Pax had been working for Mister for weeks now, and he and Kai had done many errands for him. Mister paid well—enough for food and school and even a school uniform for Kai. Soon they would be able to pay for a place to live.

"Is Mister a good man?" Kai's voice was fuzzy with sleep. He was curled up close to Pax.

"Yes, get up," said Pax.

They had old sleeping mats, a pot to carry water, a tongue-scraper, an extra T-shirt each, and a backpack. A girl named Roya protected their things when they were away. At night Pax and Kai shared their rice with her. Today they would make money. Tonight they would all eat meat.

Pax and Kai raced to their meeting place. Where was he? There were many cars about, but most were ancient and coughed like old men. Mister's car purred like a kitten.

"There he is," Kai cried out in triumph, pointing to the long, sleek car.

Pax and Kai ran towards the car. The driver opened the back door. They both jumped inside and sat across from Mister.

Mister leaned back into his cool, leather seat that squeaked like mice when he moved. He smiled, revealing brown nubs of teeth and a pale, flat tongue. "I have something for you," he said, as he took a soccer ball out of a brown paper bag.

Pax clapped his hands. Kai was excited. He squeezed his hands into fists and shook them in front of his eyes like rattles.

"Because you've done so well, I have another package for you to deliver," said Mister. The heads of both boys bobbed. "This job is simple, like the others. You will take this to a place and wait."

Mister patted a box that sat on the car seat beside him. It was different from the other boxes. This one was made of metal and sank deep into the leather seat.

"A man wearing a Western suit of clothes and a red tie— do you know what a tie is?" Mister flapped the long piece of material that hung around his own neck.

They nodded. Did he think they were stupid?

"Good. He will say to you, 'Good boys' and give you lots of coins—more than you have ever had before! Then he will take the box away.

"The driver will take you close to the spot, but after that, you will have to carry the package. This box is heavier than the last one. You must pretend that it is light. Do not hunch your shoulders." Mister bunched his shoulders up around his ears to show them what he meant. "Do not leave the box on its own. You must guard it until the man comes. Just pretend to beg."

Kai thought that rich people were stupid. Why would the man not deliver it himself? He did not know the answer and, really, he did not care.

"You take the ball. It is a gift." Mister gave Kai the beautiful black-and-white soccer ball. Kai could hardly contain his excitement. He hugged it against his chest and grinned.

Mister faced Pax. He was not smiling any more. "*You* will carry the box because you are older and stronger. Now listen to my instructions carefully."

Mister repeated the same instructions all over again. Why? Pax and Kai made their faces stop smiling, but inside they were laughing.

The car began to move. Kai reached for Pax's hand. They giggled as they pressed their faces against the window. The car cruised through the chaos of the street with ease. There were many demonstrations. People carried signs and pounded the sky with their fists. Everyone seemed angry. It was hard to understand. Twice the car drove towards mobs of people yelling. Both times the car skirted the yelling crowds.

A half-hour later they came to a new and shiny part of the city that Pax recognized. They passed the Children's Services building and the business buildings, too. The driver stopped the car.

Mister put his hand on the door handle. He was sitting on the edge of the seat. He peered at his watch. His face relaxed and he said, "We are early. Do you have any questions?"

"Yes. How much does it cost to get to England?" Pax spoke bravely.

Mister smiled, his teeth shiny with spit. "Why do you want to go to England?" he asked. Again, he looked at this watch.

"To see the Queen." Kai hugged the soccer ball.

"No. To go to school," said Pax. "Kai can read and write. He can do mathematics. He can do many things that are difficult."

Mister looked amused. "Can he? If you want to go, I will help you," he said.

Their eyes lit up. Kai cheered. Mister was looking out the window. He wasn't listening to them any more.

"Thank you," whispered Pax.

Mister looked at his watch again. "Do your job well, and after, I will see that you get to England." He got out of the car and crossed a big street. He had never done that before.

"Did you hear that? England." Kai squeezed Pax's arm.

"Yes," Pax whispered as he watched Mister disappear into the crowd. He scratched the back of his neck. He felt funny. Something felt wrong.

The driver pulled into an alley behind a great building and got out of the car. He did not speak as he opened their door, reached in, and gently pulled out the box. "Go around this building. There are steps up to the doors. Climb up to the middle of the steps and wait. It will not be long."

"How will we get home?" asked Pax.

The driver hesitated, and then said, "I will wait for you and drive you back."

The driver gave the box to Pax. It was very heavy. Pax used both hands to carry it. The box banged against his knees. Pax tried not to grunt or puff. The handle on the box was made of metal and cut into his hands. Kai followed behind, holding the ball close to his chest.

The car pulled away quickly and was soon lost in the traffic.

"Where is he going?" asked Kai.

"You heard him. Not far. He will be back," said Pax.

Nothing felt right.

They walked around the building and up the stone steps. The tall, shiny building ahead reflected sparks of colored light. Along the road, and to the side, were great, long-necked trees with huge leaves fanning out at the top.

"Here. This is where he said to wait." Pax gasped as he put the box down on a step.

Kai was careful to tuck the ball between the box and his leg so that it would not roll away. Kai held out his hand. "Pax, begging here is silly. The police will come."

Pax nodded. "Maybe the man will come soon to take the box away." Pax looked down at it. They could not run away from the police. The box was too heavy to carry far.

Chapter 20

Pax and Kai stood on the steps in front of the box, held out cupped hands, and begged for coins. They looked up at people who passed by with round, pleading eyes and hoped their stares would pierce the heart of a rich person. Everyone turned away.

There was a line of bicycle-boys on the steps a good distance away, each one standing behind or in front of a similar box. Pax did not know any of them by name but he could see one, maybe two familiar faces.

Why were they here?

Kai held the soccer ball between his ankles. "Pax, look."

A guard with keys clattering on his belt was coming towards them. He was a long way away but he was moving quickly.

"What should we do?" Kai whispered into Pax's ear.

Pax looked around. There was a man wearing a red tie approaching them from the opposite direction. Was that him? Everyone in this place seemed to wear a tie and Western suit.

He looked down the street. A crowd of people carrying signs and chanting something was moving their way.

Pax stared down at the box in front of him. The box began to make a humming noise, as if it were coming to life, as if it had been turned on. He looked at it. He looked at the boys in the distance. His head swiveled back and forth, back and forth. In that instant, Pax understood.

What should he do? Kai, he had to save Kai.

Pax snatched the soccer ball from between Kai's feet, kicked it, and yelled, "Kai, go after it!" The ball bounced down the steps, past people walking and food-sellers on the pavement. Kai let out a cheer and raced down the steps taking two, three at a time.

Now Pax waved his arms and yelled to the boys, "Away. Away!" No one paid any attention. He raced to the boy nearest him and pulled his shirt. "Get away!" he screamed.

"You'll get us in trouble!" The boy shoved Pax.

The ball rolled out onto the road and bounced off the wheel of a motorbike. Kai dodged through traffic and made it to the other side of the road.

"Kai, stay there. Don't move!" Pax stood on the pavement and screamed over the sound of the traffic. Sweat beaded on his forehead. The exhaust fumes choked him. The chanting of the mob grew louder. Pax's eyes darted every which way and then he dashed out into the traffic. He made it to the middle of the road, caught between the cars passing in opposite directions.

Kai waved at him from other side. He was yelling at Pax, but the noise all around them was too great. Kai was pointing to the box.

Pax looked back. The guard with the clattering keys who had been approaching them was now bending over the box. So what did it matter if the guard took it? Pax was never going to work for Mister again.

Pax ran out into traffic towards Kai and made it safely to the other side of the road.

"You did it!" Kai patted Pax on the back.

Pax was angry but could not talk.

He bent forward, put his hands on his knees, and tried to breathe. Nothing happened. Pax looked at the box, just a small dot on the steps. The box was fine. Bell had always said he had too big an imagination for this world. He huffed, and drew in deep breaths.

Chapter 21

The ground beneath their feet quivered. It was a shudder, a rattle, and then an earthly vomit sent millions of pounds of concrete, earth, and dust up into the sky. Then came a great gasp of wind as bodies lifted off the ground and flew about like bits of paper. Glass rained down from the surrounding buildings in great sheets, shattering and splintering as it hit the ground. The air was thick and brown.

The wind blew the boys in different directions. They were spun around in the air like balls and smacked down onto blistered cement. They lay there, feet from each other, in stunned silence. Pax looked up at the sky. The sun had been rubbed out by waves of ash.

Pax came back to himself slowly, one sense arriving at a time. First, sight.

"Kai, where are you?" Blinking madly, Pax crawled up on his hands and knees. He stood, wobbled, and fell back down.

He stood again, and this time he held his arms out straight to balance himself. He turned around and around.

"Kai, where are you?"

Was he speaking? His mouth moved but he could not hear himself. Pax whirled and twirled and got lost in the motion. He was surrounded by bodies swallowed in dust.

"Where are you?" Pax cried again and again. Dirt choked him. And then—there! Kai limped towards him. His eyes were round and wide. His hands waved, his fingers fluttered—he looked like a broken bird shot from the sky.

Pax stumbled towards him with outstretched arms and rubber legs. "I am here. I am here. I am here." He could feel his jaw go up and down and his mouth form words, but still he could not hear himself. He hit his ears with the palms of his hands. Nothing. Both ears were deaf.

Pax wrapped his arms around Kai. Trembling, Kai buried his head in Pax's chest and they sank to the ground.

Cars, bikes, taxis were just twisted rubble. Some were lying on their sides. Some were upside down with their wheels spinning. People sat frozen in their cars, hands gripping the wheel. Most of the trees were torn from the ground, their roots exposed as if giants had yanked them out of the earth with mighty hands.

A donkey lay on the road, its cheeks and nose fluttering. The animal's belly was slashed. Its insides spilled out onto the road.

The ground was splattered with brilliant red blotches. Small fires flared. People ran in all directions, clutching their heads as blood dripped through their fingers.

Broken electrical wires crackled and sparked. Pax sniffed—gasoline.

Pax pressed Kai into his chest as if to pin them together, as if to keep them both from flying away. There was nothing in his thoughts. Empty. As if his eyes and his brains had simply disconnected. They sat that way for a long time as bits of debris, paper, cloth, wafted back to the ground. Kai leaned in close. They did not cry.

Pax sniffed. The stink of gasoline from the tanks of smashed vehicles seared the inside of his nose. The gasoline, running in rivulets, met the tiny fires and burst into flames. The flames enveloped entire cars and trucks. "Get up, get away!" Pax mouthed the words to Kai, but moving was difficult.

Pax tried to stand. He held on to Kai with all his might. Everything—arms, legs, back—felt wobbly. His bones had turned to liquid. He needed something to pull himself up with, a railing, a post. There was nothing. Police cars and trucks flashed their red lights.

His hearing was coming back in bits, but as echoes, not fully formed or identifiable sounds. He stood on jelly legs. Pax pressed Kai close to his chest. How to run when he could barely walk? And where to run? Everything was upside down.

Kai turned his head. A long, sleek gun lay on the ground. All around them was dust, and yet the gun seemed to wink in a ray of filtered yellow light. Kai beat his fists against Pax's chest and pointed.

Pax couldn't think straight, and yet he could picture the three men standing in Ol' May's shack, one holding a gun. He saw Rambo with the American pistol. Now he would have a gun too.

Holding Kai with one arm, Pax bent down and wrapped his rubbery fingers around the barrel of the gun. He could defend them both now. He lifted it and tucked it under his shirt and into his pants. There was hardly anything to tuck the gun into. His clothes were in tatters and hung off him in strips.

Pax staggered down the road, Kai now on his back. Pax lurched one way and then the other. They were yellow with dust, their tongues hanging out of their mouths, throats parched, eyes round like the moon.

Chapter 22

They were arrested blocks away from the explosion site. There was shouting, threats maybe, but they sensed only vibrations from the sounds. Nothing made sense.

The gun was taken away. They were blindfolded, and their hands were tied behind their backs. Both were tossed into the back of a truck. Pax hit his head. Kai moaned as if he had suffered the blow.

They were taken to a police station. The blindfolds were taken off. Eyelids fluttering, balled-up hands rubbing sore eyes, they were photographed, fingerprinted, then shoved into a cell.

Sounds were coming back. First the sound of a cell door slamming shut, metal on metal. The sound was sharp, like a gun going off. Then they could hear words.

They sat in the cell. The floor was packed earth, the walls chalky to the touch.

"Hush, hush." Pax held Kai in his arms. He pushed his face into Kai's hair. He tried not to cry.

It was dark. No food, no water. They waited.

Later the cell door opened. The guard filled the doorway. He grabbed Pax by the arm and tossed him out into the hallway. Kai screamed. Pax tried to say something to Kai, words of comfort. A rifle butt hit Pax in the back. He fell forward. Winded, he struggled to breathe.

He was taken into a room. Table, two chairs, photographs.

"We have pictures of you on the steps with one of the bombs just before the explosion." A policeman spoke. He was large and fierce. He pounded the table and pointed to the photographs.

"Water," Pax croaked.

A paper cup was put on the table. He reached out for it. The police officer gave it a swipe. The water splashed against the wall. The policeman asked more questions, and when Pax did not answer, he repeated them again.

"Water," Pax moaned.

"You are charged with acting against national security and with spreading propaganda against the regime. That is just the beginning. Terrorism charges will also be issued against you. Unless you cooperate, you will hang," said the policeman.

Pax shook his head. What was a regime? What was propaganda?

"Kai, the boy. He is innocent," Pax whispered.

"You are part of a street gang. You worked with those who are against the regime. Give us the names of the boys in your gang."

What gang? What was he talking about? He shook his head.

The policeman yelled for a long time. He thumped down in the chair and then finally waved to the guard. "Take him away," he said.

Pax was returned to the cell.

"Pax, Pax!" Kai lifted his arms. Pax held him tight. Relief spread through Pax. At least they still had each other. He and Kai huddled together.

The cell door opened. A bowl of water was left on the floor. They lapped it up slowly. Some bread. A thin broth. Fear.

Days passed. They were given new clothes, except they were not new. There was blood on the shorts and the T-shirts did not smell good.

Again they were blindfolded and taken out of the cell and put in another truck. The drive was long. If Pax tilted his head, he could see a sliver of light above the blindfold. He saw a sleek, modern highway, billboards, road signs that had no meaning, a billboard of smiling people holding up glasses of orange liquid.

The truck slowed down and the road became bumpy. The two bounced around like rubber balls. Pax held Kai close but this time he did not say, "Hush, hush." He could not think of anything to say.

"Pax," whispered Kai.

"No talking," yelled the guard.

"Remember, you are a prince. The Prince of Light," Pax whispered back.

"Are you deaf?" The guard stabbed Pax with the muzzle of his gun just as the truck stopped.

The door of the truck opened. Two guards shouted, "Out, out, out!"

The guard in the truck yanked off their blindfolds. The light made them dizzy. They jumped down onto gravel. Kai fell. Pax reached for him.

"Don't cry," he whispered as he grabbed Kai's hand.

Pax tried to look around, take in everything at once. The prison was made of brick. It was in a forest surrounded by tall trees, short shrubs, and wildflowers.

One guard pulled them apart. Another tied Pax's arms behind his back. Pax moaned. His shoulders were nearly wrenched from their sockets.

Pax tried to whisper to Kai. He wanted to say, *Forgive me.* He wanted to say, *Do not be brave. Tell them what they want to hear.* He wanted to say, *You are the Prince of Light.*

He opened his mouth. He could see tears and snot streaming down Kai's face.

"Move!" a guard screamed.

They entered the building. A rifle butt was rammed into Pax's stomach. He fell forward, folding in half, arms behind his back, his face slamming against his knees. Pax pressed his shoulder against the wall and inched his way back up. He stood and stumbled forward, his shoulders grazing the walls.

The guards pushed them along hallways, down metal steps

and then stone steps. As they descended, the walls changed. Up top they were cool to the touch and painted white. Down below, where the metal steps turned to stone, the walls were made of rough cement and the floors were packed earth. It was cold and damp. They came to the end of a hallway. The lights were dim.

The split was sudden. One moment they were walking side by side, the next they were being pushed down different corridors.

"Pax!" Kai cried. The sound of his name echoed off the walls.

"Leave him alone. He knows nothing," Pax cried.

A door slammed. It was a mighty thud. Pax heard it in his heart, in his head, and in every fiber of his body. Kai was gone.

"Kai," Pax sobbed. He couldn't wipe the tears from his eyes, the blood from his face, or the snot running from his nose.

He was marched down a corridor. There was a railing to his left and cells to his right. The cells were holes chiseled into the walls, most no bigger than the length of a body. Some had cots, some dirty rugs on the floor, some were bare.

"Stop," bellowed the guard. Pax was shoved into a cell. "Murderer! Terrorist!" the guard growled.

Pax fell onto a thin rug that covered a mud floor. The kick to his head was unexpected, fierce, and brutal. The pain was blinding and, after that, nothing.

A day passed, perhaps two. He was given a tin cup. In the cup was a lump of green swimming in something brown.

Pax sat on the floor of his cell. If he lay out straight, his feet would touch one wall and his head would touch the other. It was no wider than the spread of his arms.

He was thirsty. His tongue was thick, his throat burned, and his insides were on fire. He didn't care about food. Water, if only he could have water. The cement cell walls were wet; they leaked like sweat through skin. He crawled over to the wall and licked it. He rubbed his face in the damp and tried to wake himself up. The light was weak, thin rays that seemed to twist down hallways and find their way into corners.

He hugged himself. He had never been alone before— ever. In the orphanage he had been surrounded by dozens of other children. When Ol' May had thrown them out onto the street, there had been Kai, and other kids too. Even mean kids were company of a kind. Always there were people around. But this—to be alone like this? It was torture.

Pax pulled his knees to his chest. "Kai," he whispered. "Don't give up. I will find you. Don't give up." It was hard to draw in air. His lungs were like stones in his chest. Teacher had said, "Ask God."

"God, keep Kai safe." It was like screaming under water.

The cries from other cells woke him—the kinds of screams a human makes when the soul is slowly ripped, stitch by stitch, from the body. There were echoes but no response.

Pax scratched the walls. "*Kai, Kai, Kai,* is that you? I am here," he cried. His nails broke and the nubs of his fingers bled. "Please God, please God, please God, don't let them hurt him."

Finally the tears stopped. There was no more water in his body for tears.

Chapter 23

*P*ax was tied to a bed, spread out on top of springs. His wrists were tied to the bedposts at the top. His legs were tied to the bedposts at the bottom.

"You were caught with a gun. You were seen with the bomb. We have witnesses. You are the leader of a gang of boys. You work for terrorists. What are their names?" the policeman demanded. But was he a policeman? It was hard to tell. He wasn't dressed like a policeman.

He wore an open-necked shirt. It was yellow with a small thing stitched on one side, an animal maybe. His pants were the sort a well-dressed tourist wore, the kind of visitor who did not give money to beggars. His shoes were made of leather, each with a small toggle that bounced back and forth as he walked. His watch was large, gold, with many dials. His hair was short and shiny. His teeth were lined up in two perfect rows. He smelled of fresh air and something sweet.

"Mister—his name was Mister. I told you this many

times." Pax spoke through clenched teeth. He had been telling them this for weeks now—maybe longer. Time had lost all meaning.

"Do you take us for fools?" asked the policeman.

Another man was in the room. He was huge, with arms like the limbs of trees, and he wore a soiled shirt, wet under the arms. Beneath a round cloth cap was a shaved skull. He had no neck. It was as if his head had been hammered directly onto his barrel-shaped torso. A long, untrimmed beard hung down his chest. He held a leather whip in one hand and stroked it with the other hand, like a pet.

He was an ogre out of a fairy story, Pax thought. A monster, made-up, silly, laughable. He would make up a story about him. His name would be Neckless. What would the story be about? He tried to put his mind someplace else, someplace far, far away.

The policeman nodded to Neckless. Pax pulled at the restraints. He waited for the blow. Neckless lifted the whip and slashed his feet. The pain seared the inside of his body.

"Mister? What is his full name?" asked the policeman-torturer.

"I don't know." Pax's words lodged in his throat.

"Where does he live?" he shouted.

"I don't know." How was he to know such a thing?

The whip came down, again. With each stroke, Pax thought he might slip into oblivion. Not death, he did not want to die. He had to save Kai. He wanted to go to a place where there was no pain. *Think. Think.*

"Tell us about the street gang of boys," said the policeman.

Pax gnashed his teeth. "I am not part of a gang," he answered.

"LIAR! You are a liar. LIAR. LIAR. Even now we are rounding up the boys on the street. Do you know the boy called Rambo? He tells us that you were the leader of the gang. What of the boy Tirta? He tells us that you are a thief."

The whip came down, again.

Pax screamed. This time blood flew up and spattered Neckless.

The policeman stepped aside. He examined his shirt, then took out a white handkerchief and dabbed at a spot of blood. He looked at his watch.

"This foreign man named Andy gave you a bicycle. How was he involved?" The policeman suddenly sounded tired.

"He was not involved," said Pax.

"Then you were involved."

"I don't understand."

Over and over Pax tried to think of a story about Neckless. Perhaps he was a dwarf-giant from another planet. That's it. Everyone around him was a giant but he was little. He had been banished to Earth.

"You said this . . . *Andy* was not involved. That means that *you* were involved, or how would you know? Tell us the names of the people who are terrorists. Confess that you are the leader of a street gang of boys who plotted to kill." The policeman's words were loud, but at the same time he sounded rather bored—as if he was weary of the questions.

"I do not understand." How could he be a leader of anything?

"Tell me if you recognize any of these names." The policeman read out names of men and women Pax had never heard of or met.

He tried to imagine Neckless in a sea of giants. Maybe they came from the ocean? The story was receding, drifting away. It wasn't a very good story . . .

The man leaned down and hissed in Pax's ear. "I will tell you something. The feet are the most sensitive part of the body. This will happen again and again. You will get a daily ration of fifty lashes until you confess that you are the leader of street boys who plotted to kill. Even now we are rounding up more street boys. In the end, they will all say that you are their leader."

Again and again and again. The blows to his feet created a trail of flames that licked his legs, raced up his spine, and exploded in his head. He was being roasted alive from the inside out. No story could control it, reduce it, or charm it away.

Later Pax was forced to walk back down the hallway. He left bloody footprints down the halls.

"It's good for the circulation, to get the blood to your feet. Otherwise your feet will get infected and we will have to cut them off," said the guard who shuffled behind him. He too seemed bored.

Pax was taken to a new cell. He clutched the doorframe with his hands and tried to hobble forward. On the mud floor of his cell was a thick mat and two pillows. Pillows? Where had they come from?

Pax fell forward. He put one pillow under his head and the second under his feet.

Sleep was impossible. The pain in his feet arrived in waves. Every wave was like a jolt of electricity. The noise in the prison was constant: banging, rattling, yelling, clinking, cell doors opening and closing, metal scraping metal. There was screaming, too. It echoed up and down the halls, bounced off walls, and stuck to him like sweat.

He heard footsteps, great, clobbering steps that a giant might make. There was the sliding of a bolt, the turning of a key, and a rumble.

"Get up."

Pax rolled onto all fours. Slowly, using the wall, he stood. He came out of the cell like a rabbit, nose first, body trembling. He stumbled down a hall. Every step shot rivers of pain up his legs and into his head.

"You have five minutes in the toilet." The guard hovered above him, his breath stale and smelly.

Pax hobbled down the hall and vomited into a stinking hole.

When Pax returned to his cell, there was a tin cup filled with broth. His hand shook as he held the cup up to his mouth. He drank it all.

He fell asleep.

There was an announcement on the loudspeaker. They called his name. He was not awake, but he was not asleep either. He was in that place where pain invades the mind and leaves one paralyzed.

His cell door opened. A guard stood on the threshold.

This guard was different from the last. He did not wear a uniform. He was in rags but he carried a big stick.

"Did you not hear your name? GET UP!" he shouted.

Pax lay on his side. The guard slammed his stick down on Pax's waist and something deep inside his body broke. Pax moaned.

"When you hear your name on the loudspeaker, you must go to interrogation," screamed the guard.

Hand over hand, Pax clawed his way up. He stood and looked at the person holding the stick. A tongue coated in a thick white film flicked against black teeth. The teeth stuck out of rotting gums like crooked tombstones poking out of the ground. He was wearing a long, dirty shirt that came down to his knees. His pants were torn. His knees bulged like knotted ropes under scabby skin stretched too tight.

"You are a pretty boy. Wait. You will not have that face much longer. If you do not hurry, they will make it worse for you." The guard poked him with the stick.

"Kai, the boy, where is he?" said Pax.

"Who is this Kai?"

"He is a boy. He came with me to this place. Where is he?" Pax tried to be brave, tried to stand tall.

"What have you got to give me?" asked the ragged guard.

"I have nothing."

"Then I have nothing to tell you." The stick swiped Pax's back. "Hurry up."

Pax shuffled down the corridor.

Chapter 24

This interrogation was no different from the last, and the one before it. How many? Pax had lost count. He would tell them what they wanted, but he knew nothing. They wanted him to say that Andy was a terrorist. Andy? Who was Andy? It was hard to remember things. Pax said nothing because there was nothing to say.

Pax stumbled back to his cell. Again, the tin cup was full and beside it was a hunk of bread. His hands shook as he held the cup to his lips. He chewed the bread slowly. He fell into a black, dreamless sleep.

Light from the hallway came into his cell. His tongue thick, his mouth parched, he reached for his tin cup. He whispered, "Let there be a drop left, just a drop." It was a prayer.

"Looking for this?" The raggedy guard stood on the threshold holding up a lamp, and for a moment Pax thought of Bell. How she hated it when people stood in doorways. "It's bad luck," she would say. Bell, Bell, Bell. *Help me, Bell.* A silent prayer.

"What are you mumbling?" snapped the raggedy guard. Pax shook his head.

The guard reached for Pax's tin cup. "I said, what are you mumbling?" He growled like a dog as he threw the cup at Pax. "Answer me!" The stick came down on Pax's head.

Pax fell back into darkness.

He divided night from day not by light but by sounds. During the day there was screaming. At night he could hear sobs. Now, it was night.

There was someone in his cell. Pax held his breath. His ears perked. Shuffling. He felt a hand cup the back of his head.

"Sit up," the voice hissed in his ear.

Pax struggled to sit. He heard the word "Drink."

Pax felt cool water run down his throat. His parched lips were moistened.

"M-more," Pax stammered.

Again, water was dribbled into his mouth. "Sip slowly." Who was talking? Looking out through his swollen eyes was like peering through dirty water.

"Who are you?" Pax asked.

"My name is Ezat. Sip more water. Not too fast." More cool liquid dripped down his throat. "Tell me your name," he asked.

Questions. Pax did not like questions. But the man offered water. He seemed—kind. Was it a trick?

"Pax," he mumbled.

"Listen to me, Pax. The one who was beating you with the stick—he is a *repentant*, a prisoner who does the bidding of the guards. They call him Stink Boy. They give him extras— food, clothes, cigarettes, money—to be a bully. Do as he says. He isn't much older than you are. How old are you? This is important. They execute boys over fifteen."

"I am almost fifteen" he answered. The truth was, he no longer knew exactly how old he was. "Can you help me find Kai? He is only a boy. He will be a mathematician one day and go to a great university."

"Eat. I brought you bread," said Ezat.

With only meager light from the hallway, Pax's eyes drifted from cup to bread to the face of the man above him. He'd said his name was Ezat.

Ezat stood and turned to the cell door, peering left, then right. He moved like a soldier—shoulders back, head held high—but he was crooked all the same, sloped to one side. He was tall and skinny. His dark hair was mixed with white.

"Why are you helping me?" asked Pax. His voice was raspy.

The man returned to Pax's side. "I have a son. He is younger than you, just a baby. He is with his mother. I hope that maybe someone will help them. I do not have much time. Listen."

Ezat went back to the doorway and once again peered up and down the hall before sitting back down beside Pax.

"There are men in here who will take care of you, good men. Political prisoners. I must not stay too long. The guards watch. They will think we are plotting. Come out to the common room. We can help you there. You too are a political prisoner. Do you know what that means?" asked Ezat.

Pax shook his head.

"You are not allowed visitors. You will be kept separate. They will torture you. During torture they will read out names. If you identify any of those names, they will do to them what they are doing to you. Do you understand?"

Pax nodded.

"You are a boy, but that won't protect you. If you are to survive—are you listening? If you are to survive, you must think of other things—stories, good times, happy memories. You must let your mind help protect you." Ezat looked down at Pax with soft eyes.

Pax stared up at the man. Yes, yes, he knew about stories. He understood stories. He tried to make up a story about Neckless. Pain cuts through stories.

They both heard footsteps.

"I will come back." Ezat vanished.

Where did he go? Had he imagined him?

Pax fell back into a dreamless sleep.

Chapter 25

Pax was asleep, but not a deep sleep, not a restful sleep. He was ready, at any moment, to protect himself.

Stink Boy raised his baton and smacked it hard against Pax's shoulder. "Wake up, Prison Boy. Your little friend is with the guards. They like him very much." Stink Boy laughed.

A surge of energy flooded his body. Pax leapt up. His hands reached for Stink Boy's throat. Stink Boy slammed his stick against Pax's chest. Pax gasped, fell back against the wall, and slid to the ground.

"Now you are awake! Maybe he is not with the guards. Maybe he is being beaten at this moment." Stink Boy stood over him and chuckled.

Pax's chest contracted. He pulled his knees up to his chin. What had he done? No one would come for him. No one would come for Kai. It was his fault. If he had never thought about England, about Kai going to a faraway school, he would not have been blinded by the money Mister offered. If Kai died, he would be responsible for his death. It was easier to think him dead than to imagine him being abused, being passed from man to man, being tortured. If he was dead, he would be out of reach, out of pain, out of harm's way.

"Kai, forgive me," Pax howled, like an animal in a trap.

"Quiet! They will call for you soon. You should tell them what they want to hear." Stink Boy rapped his stick against the cell doors as he left. *Bang, bang, bang.*

Pax waited to be called over the loudspeaker. Waiting was the worst. He tried not to cry, but the tears felt good in his eyes. He lay down.

"Pax?"

Who was calling him? Pax lifted his head and perked his ears as he rubbed the wet from his face. He listened.

"Pax."

It was Ezat. He entered the cell and sat beside Pax.

"This was smuggled in." Ezat spread a newspaper on the floor.

Pax crawled towards Ezat on his knees. He should try to stand. They said that walking was good for his circulation and would eventually toughen the soles of his feet, but the pain was excruciating.

Pax looked down at the front page of the newspaper. He recognized himself. "It's me! Kai too. Where did it come from?" The picture was startlingly clear, their faces looking forward as if staring into the camera.

"It looks like it is from a security camera. They are popular in that part of the city," said Ezat.

Above the photograph it said, "Terrorists held in custody."
Under the picture it said, "Street Boys Become Boy Terrorists."

"We are not terrorists," Pax whispered. He tried to read
the article beneath the photograph, but the paper was badly
crumpled. It might have said, "22 killed in timed explosions,
108 wounded."

"I am not a killer, and Kai is just a boy." Vomit rose up in
his throat. "They think I set a bomb, that I deliberately killed
people." Pax turned away.

"No, Pax. You are too young and know too little. You
were being used. And you are being used still." Ezat folded his
legs under him.

"I do not understand. How can they use me still?" Pax
looked at Ezat.

"They have not caught the men responsible for the
bombings. Some say the government set off the bombs. They
say that the government needed an excuse to clean up the
streets," said Ezat.

"How can they blame the street kids?" Pax's voice was
raspy.

"It does no good to think too much about that. You must
use all your strength to survive. You are not alone. There
are people on the outside who are trying to help you. There
are good people in this country." Ezat was gentle, his voice
almost comforting.

"Who?" There was no one in the whole world who cared
about him or Kai.

"It's best if you do not know, that way you cannot tell.
Remember, you are not alone. It is possible that if you are put

on trial, the world will see that you are just a boy, that it was not you who planned this destruction," said Ezat.

"But what if the judge and the government don't care about what the world thinks?" asked Pax. "What if I am found guilty?"

Ezat shook his head. "It is hard to tell what will happen. A government in disarray is like a cornered rat, it is hard to predict what it will do."

Inside Pax's head he screamed, *This is unfair. I did nothing!* But his lips did not move. He turned his head to the wall. Trial. Execution. He remembered Kai coming back from the execution, Ol' May walking behind him. Kai had said that the hanged man kicked his feet as the rope choked the life out of him. He died kicking his feet in the air—dancing. Pax closed his eyes.

"Come out. Come and meet the others. You must try, Pax. You will gain strength from the others. They understand." Ezat offered his hand to help him up.

Pax lay on the mat and shook his head. It was better to be alone, better to hide, better to sleep.

Ezat put a finger to his lips. Both heard the *thud-thud* of Stink Boy as he lumbered down the hallway. The sound echoed from a long way off. Ezat folded the newspaper and tucked it under his shirt.

"Remember what I said. Go to a place in your mind where you can find peace. Your brain controls your limbs, your eyes, your thoughts." Ezat leaned in closer. "Use your imagination. Let it take you far away. Exercise your body as best you can. Find a place in your body that does not hurt, a shoulder, a hand—something. Exercise it. Make that part of your body stronger. This is how you fight back. Will you do that?" he asked.

Pax nodded. He wasn't listening. He was thinking, *What happens to people when they die? Where do they go? Do sins go with them?*

Ezat left quietly and, once he was gone, Pax cried.

Chapter 26

Pax lay on the bed, his hands and feet tied. The policeman who dressed like a tourist sat beside him on a chair. "Do you want this to stop?" he whispered in Pax's ear. *Yes, yes, more than anything.* Pax nodded. "I do not want to hurt you. I want the truth," said the policeman.

"I have told you all that I know," said Pax. The man ran his hands through his hair. Pax turned his head. For the first time Pax looked at him, really looked. The man had soft eyes. How could that be?

"Because of your actions, many people are dead and over a hundred no longer have limbs, are blind, cannot hear. Your boss caused this. My boss wants answers. The people want answers. They want to be kept safe. If making a boy tell the truth will help keep them safe, then that is what the government will do. It is not my fault. I must do what I am told. Do you understand?" said the policeman. He was speaking in a normal voice now.

"I understand," said Pax.

"Then tell me the truth."

"I have told you all that I know." Tears choked him. He coughed.

"That is the problem. I don't believe you." The policeman sighed.

The days passed. Pax seldom left his cell, despite Ezat's insistence. Some days he was beaten. On the other days he was left to think about being beaten. He no longer tried to make up stories about Neckless. The pain of being beaten cut like jagged teeth through any thoughts or stories or happy memories. Ezat was wrong. His imagination brought no relief. He rubbed his side. There was a dull pain there, a different pain from all the rest.

As he lay curled up on the thin mat, he felt something. There was a bump underneath the mat. It was not there before. Where did it come from?

Pax pulled himself up, pushed the thin rug aside, and ran his hand across the mud floor. A small beam of light from the hall fell directly on the bump—as though he was being led to it. He scratched at the dirt. He felt something, or rather the tip of something. He pulled at it. Dirt loosened and flew up into his face. A book! Who would bury a book in a cell? He dusted it off and held it up to the light.

The book was covered in soft leather. It was red and black. He opened it and took a quick breath. Pictures, beautiful pictures! For a moment he was in another place, another time.

Maybe it was a sign from God that Kai was all right. That was it. It had to be true. "Kai, be alive. Be safe."

Bang, bang, bang. Stink Boy was coming back. Pax put the book behind him and pressed it against the cell wall. He pulled his knees up to his chest and hugged them.

"What are you doing?" Stink Boy stood at the cell door. His words curled around Pax like smoke.

"Nothing," said Pax.

"Why are you sitting like that?"

"My back hurts."

"What do you have there?" Stink Boy stepped into the cell and held his stick over Pax's head.

"Nothing." Pax flinched.

"Liar." Stink Boy waved the stick threateningly.

Pax raised his hand to protect himself. Stink Boy grabbed hold of Pax's arm and hurled him against the far wall. Pax cried out.

"Ha!" Stink Boy held the treasure.

"I found it. It is mine." Pax lurched forward.

"Pah! Not for you. Have you learned nothing?" Stink Boy laughed. He held the book above Pax's head. Pax leapt. His arms slashed the air like spinning pinwheels.

"Nothing is yours in this place, not even your soul." The crippled hand of Stink Boy came down hard on Pax's head. Pax reeled. "Ha, ha, ha. You think you can hurt me? You are piss in the ground." Frothy spittle dripped from the corner of Stink Boy's mouth. He was sick, like the dogs in the street. He wiped his face with a filthy hand and opened the book. That was Pax's moment. He reached up and tried to snatch it back.

Stink Boy yanked it upwards. A picture tore out of the book. Pax held it in his hand. He gasped. He hadn't meant to hurt the book.

"That's all you get." Stink Boy growled. He sniffed the air, tucked the book under his arm, and ran down the hall, hugging the walls like a rat.

Pax crumpled to the ground, but for the first time in weeks he felt good. He had attacked Stink Boy and he was still alive. That was something.

He uncurled his fist. The picture was crumpled. Pax laid it out on the rug and rolled the heel of his palm across the page. He held the page out to try to capture the light from the grimy window. The bars of light created stripes on the picture. Pax rubbed his eyes and tried to clear away the mist that coated them like rain on a window. He squinted.

The picture was beautiful. It was the most beautiful thing he had ever seen, ever imagined. What was it? Had he seen it before? Large feathered wings fanned out across the page. It was a bird with the face of a young girl. Her head was covered with a cap of crested diamonds. Her eyes were sparkly, like white pebbles under blue water. Jewels were woven into her feathers.

"I know you," he whispered. It was the poster he had peeled away from a wall. "You are a princess. No, you are a goddess! You are *Goddess Girl*."

Pax lifted the picture to his face. Her feathered wings were as soft as silk. The jewels of her crown were as smooth as river rocks. He petted the wings and felt them flutter in his hand.

PRISON BOY • 161

Wait, he could feel the feathers. They were white—he had never seen such white, never felt *white*.

He wove his fingertips in and out of the speckled feathers.

"What are you doing?"

Who spoke? He looked to the door. He looked up to the window. It was a girl's voice. No, girls would not be allowed in the prison, at least he had never heard of any.

"Are you deaf?"

Pax dropped the picture and lurched backwards as if slapped. She spoke!

"I said, why are you touching me?" She stood right in front of him now. She lifted her giant wings. They were big, much bigger than the cell.

"Can you speak?" Suddenly her wings folded together behind her and formed a long, glittering, splendid tail.

Speak?

Crab-like, Pax scurried into the corner of the cell. He cowered.

"What are you afraid of? Have you done something wrong?" Goddess Girl hovered over him.

Pax shook his head. He had done nothing wrong.

"Are you stupid?"

Pax shook his head again, but faster.

"I do not like stupid boys. Prove to me that you are not stupid."

He sat up straight, his back pressed hard against the cold cement wall. How was he to prove such a thing?

"Do you want to fly?" she asked.

Fly? He nodded, dumbly.

"You may be stupid. I will decide later. Do you want to get out of here?"

Yes, yes. Who would not? He nodded again, this time vigorously, his head bobbing on its spindly stem. "But . . . what are you?" he whispered, the words hardly audible.

"So you do speak. This is an improvement. What am I? What are *you*?" She was incredulous.

"I am a boy . . . I am an orphan . . . I have no parents . . . I am alone except for Kai. I live here, in prison." He felt ashamed, guilty.

"What is your name?"

"Pax, Paxton, but here they call me Prison Boy."

"Is Prison Boy your name?" she asked.

Pax shook his head.

"Then why do you use it? Are you sure that you are not stupid?"

He nodded. No, he shook his head. He was confused. He couldn't think of what to do.

"I will call you Young King. Well, Young King, if you are alone and forgotten, you have nothing to lose." She turned her back to him. Her feathered tail fanned out to fill a room ten, twenty, a hundred times the size of his cell.

"Hurry. I do not like to be kept waiting."

How should he do this? He took a tentative step. His feet were dirty. He put a toe on a feather.

"Really, I am quite bored."

She spoke but did not turn around. What if Stink Boy came back right at that moment? Would he hurt her?

"You have one more chance," said Goddess Girl.

And so Pax, Prison Boy, Young King climbed onto the feathery back of Goddess Girl, part bird, part girl. He pressed his face against her feathered head, wrapped his arms around her long, soft neck, hugged her body with his legs and felt lift. *Swoosh!*

They rose above the prison, the bushes, the flowers, the trees. The ground below grew small, smaller, smaller still. Warm air washed him. He felt clean. He felt no pain. He laughed, and the wind whitened his teeth. Up and up they soared. The clouds formed little pillow islands. Between them spots of sunlight danced wildly. Higher still the soft clouds buffered prickly air. The air turned cool.

Pax burrowed down into Goddess Girl's downy feathers. He had never been so warm. He heard her wings slap against the air. He felt her heart beat, her muscles pulse, and blood pump through her body. He closed his eyes and fell into a deep, restful sleep.

When he awoke a little later, he felt calm and unafraid. He worked his way up through Goddess Girl's feathers and sat on her back, tall and proud. The ground below had long since disappeared. The clouds too had vanished. All that was left was sunlight, great streams of brilliant light. Pax blinked and shielded his eyes as Goddess Girl skirted the sun.

"Where are we going?" he cried. The words flew back into his face. He tried again. "Where are we going?" he yelled.

Goddess Girl settled on an air current, turned her long swan neck back, and peered at him with cobalt-blue eyes. "Look," she said.

Pax gazed down at a white sandy beach. The sand rose in waves like the ocean before it. Each grain of sand twinkled and beckoned. They landed in a swoop, Goddess Girl tucking her wings in neatly.

Pax slid off Goddess Girl's back and looked around with wonder. In front of him was a great sea, the water first blue, then green as the waves reached up and caught the reflection of the sun. The ice-white caps that tipped the waves became translucent before they again fell back into the blue water.

What was this place? As Pax stood, wide-eyed with wonder, a great swell of water rose up. Out of the sea came whales and tuna, sharks and minnows. Dolphin chatter infused the air.

He felt something. It surged through him with such speed it left him breathless with wonder, and on its heels . . . happiness.

They called his name on the loudspeaker. Pax opened his eyes. The pain had returned.

Chapter 27

"Pax, listen carefully," said Ezat. They sat in the common room, cross-legged on the floor. Rugs were scattered on top of the unforgiving, cold, damp cement. There were no tables, no chairs, no lamps or bookcases. Nothing.

Pax looked at Ezat. Should he tell him about Goddess Girl? Would he believe him? No, he would wait. And anyway, she had not returned for days, no matter how many times he called out to her. Perhaps she would never come back.

Pax sat in a circle of men. All were much older than him and all were political prisoners. All were kind to him. All had bandaged feet, scarred backs, broken bones that had healed at odd angles.

Each prisoner held a piece of bread; each sipped from a tin cup. Hands quivered, liquid sloshed, loose teeth chewed slowly. Today there were vegetables floating in the cups, along with flies and bugs.

Pax sat up as tall as he could. The effort sent waves of throbbing pain up and down his spine. He cringed and said nothing. He wanted to be worthy of the other men's company.

"This is Ebrahim. He is a great artist, a sculptor. The government feared his hands," said Ezat.

Pax looked at Ebrahim through blurry eyes. The man was not very old, although it was hard to tell. His hair was white, his skin a patchwork of sores. There were large welts on his ankles and wrists where he had been chained. Pax tried not to look at his hands, but it was no use. They were mangled, gnarled, his fingers attached at an odd angle, his fingernails curled and split around the tips. His hand had been smashed.

Ebrahim followed Pax's gaze and he too looked down at his hands. "I am an artist, not in my hands but in my soul. They have yet to destroy my soul. Would you like to make some art?" he asked Pax.

"Art? In this place?" Pax's eyebrows shot up in surprise.

Ebrahim nodded and smiled. It was a strange sight, a man smiling in this place. "Here, take my bread. Take the inside of the bread, the softest part. Wet it with the soup, not too much. Now mold it into a tiny sculpture," said Ebrahim.

"See, I have one." Ezat pulled a tiny, perfect bird from his pocket. Pax almost cried out in delight. It was a beautiful thing. "One of the guards gives our small art pieces to the women, and their babies and children, who live in the prison."

"Babies? Children?" Pax's eyes widened.

"They are on the other side of the wall." Ezat shook his head slowly.

"Why?" Pax flinched.

"Why are they here? Is that what you are asking? The wives of political prisoners are innocent. What have they done except to marry the wrong man?" Ezat suddenly fell silent and swallowed several times.

Pax gazed around the circle. Heads hung low. Ezat had said that they were all political prisoners. Where were their wives and children?

"Others are in prison because they stole to feed their families," Ebrahim added. "Some may simply have run away from husbands or family members who beat them. They were caught and charged with made-up crimes. There are other women here to carry out the sentences of their husbands or brothers. Or perhaps a man is sick of his wife and so he tells the judge that she was seen talking to another man."

"I don't understand," whispered Pax.

"Which part?" Ezat asked.

"All of it."

Ebrahim gently touched Pax's knee. It was a signal. A guard was near. For a few moments all fell silent. When the danger passed, it was Ezat who spoke. It was as if the two men were taking turns teaching him.

"And there are young girls, too," said Ezat.

"Girls?" Pax thought of Mega. How would she survive in such a place?

Ezat's voice was now calm and teacher-like. "Some girls try to stand up for their rights. They might want to go to school or learn how to drive a car. Perhaps they were caught protesting, or simply writing an essay in school about women's rights. A teacher or another student might report them to the authorities. They will be held in prison for weeks, perhaps months. Once they are released, their families will likely not accept them back. They have brought shame to their family. They are tainted, their reputations compromised."

"But what about the courts? A judge would let them go!" No matter how hard he tried, Pax could not get his head around it.

"Many girls or women will never enter a courtroom, talk to a lawyer, or even see a judge," said Ezat.

"But why are there babies and little children in here?" asked Pax. It was impossible. It was—inhuman.

The baton had been passed again. It was Ebrahim's turn to speak. "If a mother is jailed, she might plead with her family or her husband's family to take the child. If they say no, the child is brought to jail with her."

"But what about putting the child in an orphanage?" Pax whispered.

"Most are full." Ebrahim shrugged.

Yes, yes, Pax remembered the woman who came to the Pink House with her clipboard. He remembered her words exactly: "I am from Children's Services. Our great King has decided that people like you should go back to your own country and take care of your own orphans." The government did not want to spend money on orphans. What good were they?

"What happens to the children . . . in here . . . ?" Pax spoke softly, as if he didn't really want to hear the answer.

"They are not fed properly. They have no diapers, no blankets, no toys or books. They are criminals without having committed a crime," said Ezat. He spoke calmly, without emotion.

Pax said nothing. He dabbed the bread with soup and fiercely molded it into a shape. He was hungry. It was hard not to swallow the bread.

"Is there a way to find out if there is a boy on the other side of the wall? His name is Kai."

Ezat nodded. "You asked once before. No one had heard of him, but I will try again."

A bell rang. The men rose, each helping the other to stand. One by one, they stood. Knees popped, feet shuffled. No one complained. Pax tucked his little piece of art into his pocket and hobbled over to the wall that divided the men from the women. Damp seeped out of the cement to form a gritty layer of sweat that dripped in tracks down the wall.

Pax pressed his palms, his nose, his face against the wall. His chest heaved up and down, up and down, until he was breathless. His tears mixed with the damp.

"God, where are you? Help us," he sobbed.

"Prison Boy, back to your cell." Stink Boy stood behind him.

Pax rubbed his face with the back of his hand, pulled back his shoulders, turned, and hobbled across the common room towards the hall that led to his cell.

Chapter 28

"**H**ey, Prison Boy." Stink Boy stepped into the cell and poked Pax with his stick. "Come with me," he commanded.

"But my name was not announced over the loudspeaker." Pax was not as frightened as he had once been. The beatings were hardening him, and he had shown no sign of betraying anyone.

"Do not ask questions!"

Stink Boy yanked Pax to his feet and put a blindfold over his eyes. The blindfold was tight. It pushed his eyes back into their sockets.

Stink Boy guided Pax down the hall with guttural sounds and a stick. The screech of a cell door opening and closing was as distinctive as glass breaking on a hard floor. He held his arms out in front of him, searching, searching, his hands pedaling the air. He stumbled. He bounced off the walls. He fell and pulled himself up. The pain in his side was increasing.

"They will come for you when they are ready."

Stink Boy pushed him into a room. It reeked of vomit, dried blood, and excrement. He tied Pax's arms behind his back, wrenching his shoulders. Pax sat and waited.

Waiting was painful. Waiting was the real torture, worse than a beating. A beating, once started, would eventually be over, or he would be dead. But waiting went on and on.

He felt a brush of feathers against his skin.

"Come. This is no place for you."

The blindfold fell from his eyes. His hands were untied. He felt light. There was no pain in his feet, his back. His whole body was suddenly, instantly, pain-free.

"Do not keep me waiting. I simply hate being kept waiting. It is so frightfully boring." Goddess Girl flapped her giant wings.

"Yes, I am coming." Pax climbed onto the back of Goddess Girl and, in a heartbeat, floors, walls, ceilings disappeared.

It was morning. The sun sparkled. The air was fresh. Pax sat up on Goddess Girl's back and looked up at the clear blue sky.

"Sleep now, Young King. I will wake you when we arrive." Goddess Girl threw back her jeweled head and soared heavenward.

"Where are we going?" he yelled into the wind.

"To a place that will bring you peace. Sleep."

Pax burrowed deep into Goddess Girl's soft down, curled into a ball, and slept. He slept for a long time, deeply and peacefully. He had a dream.

"Kai, are you safe?" he called out. And just as a prayer sometimes returns as a song, he heard, "I love you."

"Wake now. We are here," said Goddess Girl.

"Where are we?" Pax emerged from under her feathers. The wings of Goddess Girl flapped slowly. She circled below the clouds and above an ivory-white coast.

Pax rubbed his eyes and looked down upon a winding river. He could see clearly. The wind was warm. The banks of the river were dry.

"Here is the source of all the salt in the universe. Here the unfortunate come to weep their salty tears. Here they will cry oceans of tears and always be thirsty," said Goddess Girl as she slowly flapped her wings.

"Why have you brought me here? Is it because this is where I belong?" said Pax.

"No, you do not belong here, Young King. Others belong here, but not you."

Again Goddess Girl flapped her wings and up they went. They skimmed over the land and floated above a lake. Pax peered over her shoulder and stared into a clear pool of still water.

"Look, it's me!" he cried.

There were no marks on him, no welts where he had been beaten. His eyes were not black, his lips were not swollen and cracked. He looked at his legs and feet. The skin was not hanging off. His feet were whole. His stomach was full although he had eaten no food, and best of all, the pain in his side was gone.

Goddess Girl dove towards the riverbank at breakneck speed. Pax cried out in both fright and delight. Moments before they might crash, Goddess Girl pulled up and sang out, her voice echoing across the sky. It was a strange sound, not human, more like sweet music sung by millions upon millions of fireflies.

They landed on the sandy bank. She turned her long, swan-like neck towards him. Her eyes glistened like sapphires. "We must wait," she said.

"Why?" asked Pax.

"You will be judged in front of a court. Is it not what you wanted? To be judged fairly?"

Pax reeled back. "Yes. No. What will happen?" He was confused.

"You will see," said Goddess Girl. She folded her wings behind her. "Look up!"

Pax drew in a deep breath. The sky was filled with wings. He opened his mouth to speak. No words came out. He looked first to one side, and then the other. There were hundreds, no, thousands upon thousands of winged goddesses. Light bounced off their wings. Feathers and jewels shimmered, giving off rays of color. The colors filled his eyes. What were they called? The names of colors he knew came from the crayons Bell's sister sent from England—sun-glow, sea green, razzle-dazzle rose. None were right. He needed more words, better words.

The expanse of their crystal wings filled the air. Their jewel-encrusted bodies winked and blinked in the light. The movement of the wings created a thin, beguiling song, a hum, a trill.

As if pulled by an invisible thread, Pax slid off the back of Goddess Girl and stood alone on the ivory-white sand. A throng of goddesses quickly surrounded him.

One goddess, more powerful and more astonishing than all the rest, came forward. Her eyelids glittered with diamonds; her eyes were the color of honey. She shone from within and without. She threw back her head and sang out, a beautiful lilting cry. The singing stopped. All went quiet.

The great goddess spoke. "My name is Queen Alzara. We know about you, Young King. We know of your hardships. You will answer my questions, and my court of goddesses will be your judges."

She peered down from on high and addressed only Pax. *"Might and right.* Tell me what these words mean to you, Young King."

King? He was not a king! He felt tiny in the face of all this magnificence. He dithered, he wobbled.

"I am waiting for an answer," said the great goddess.

What was the answer? And what were the consequences if he got it wrong? *Might*—the guards of the prison had might. They used their power and their might to hurt. Might, misused, was not right.

And then a voice came from within. *Do what's right with all your might.* Pax said it softly out loud. He looked around and stared into the honey-black eyes of the goddesses. The goddesses nodded.

"That is correct. Might must be used for right. Do you have regrets?" asked the great goddess.

Pax nodded. "Yes." He could not tell a lie.

"What do you regret?" she asked.

"I did not want Kai and me to be separated. I should have let the soldiers take him. He would be in school now." He was ashamed.

"And so you can tell the future?" she asked.

Pax said nothing.

"This boy, this Kai, why did you want to keep him with you?"

"To keep him safe, to see that he went to school. I did neither."

"You were ambitious."

Pax did not know what that word meant.

"I do not know."

"Are you faithful?"

Pax nodded. "I think so."

"Yes or no?"

"Yes."

"The ambitious climb, the faithful build. You wanted to help this boy build a future. Have no regrets, Young King. Are you mean in your heart?"

Pax pulled back, astonished. "No, never."

"Are you a thief?"

He looked down at his feet. He took the gun. He took Bell's money box.

He nodded.

"Shall I tell you what a thief is? A thief is someone who takes and takes but never has enough. There is always more to steal, more to covet, more to hide away in dark places. A thief takes what he cannot use and keeps it from those in need. A thief never gives freely, but only under obligation. A thief steals more than things; he steals what those things represent—memories, love, history, power. I ask you again, are you a thief?"

Pax shook his head.

"Are you loyal?"

He would die for Kai. Pax nodded.

"Good. Loyalty leads to bravery. It is the foundation of all that is good, kind, and true. It is fueled by integrity and love. Now I will tell you, fight to live. Fulfill your purpose. But do not fear death." Again she held her head high, flapped her wings, and cried out in a voice that echoed across the galaxies, "HEAR ME. I pronounce this boy free of any crime."

The song of the clapping wings was sweet and high. He wanted to say thank-you, but in a swoop the goddesses flew up and up and plunged back into the clouds. Their sparkle remained in the sun's rays.

Pax lifted his arms, to wave good-bye but also as a faint plea to join them, to fly with them. He turned. In an instant panic overwhelmed him. Had he been deserted? Where was she? Pax shaded his eyes, searching, searching for the goddess who had brought him here, *his* goddess.

"I am here, Young King." She flew towards him.

His heart leapt at the sound of her voice, at the color of her eyes. They were blue, the color of the ocean, different from all the rest. Pax climbed on her back and burrowed under her feathers.

Up they went, soaring and plunging, twisting and turning. And then the sky turned a shimmering, twinkling, sparkling midnight blue. The sky was full of giant birds. Their beaks were golden, their eyes ruby red. Great wings beat the air, glowing and sending off flares of light.

"Who are they?" cried Pax.

"They are soldiers who command the skies and protect our domain."

In an instant they were flying beside Goddess Girl and Pax, their wings beating in rhythm. The lead soldier turned his head. His beak was gold, his feathers slick. He lowered his head and soared.

"Will I be a soldier who can fly?" cried Pax.

"All things will become possible. Hold on." Goddess Girl surged ahead. "As strong and powerful as the young soldiers are, they will never beat me!" Her laughter was like song.

Away they flew.

"Boy, wake." Stink Boy poked him with his stick. "It is time."

Chapter 29

"Pax, follow my voice. Come back."

"Ezat? Is that you?" Pax's voice was rough. Forming words hurt.

"I am here." Ezat kneeled beside him. He held the cup of water to Pax's lips.

"Kai, did you find him? Is he safe?" The water felt cool on his lips and in his throat.

"There is no word on him," said Ezat.

Pax pulled himself up onto his elbows. No word? Was he dead? A scream caught in his throat. "Where could he be?"

"Lie back. Think of yourself now. There is a doctor in the prison. He was just arrested. He is one of us. I have asked him to come." Ezat adjusted the thin pillow under Pax's head.

"Doctor?" Pax nodded and fell back onto the mat that lay on the floor of his cell. Water dribbled down the side of his face and into his hair. "Why is a doctor in such a place?" whispered Pax.

"He is a political prisoner like us. He hid a good man in his home. That man was a reporter, a writer. To be a reporter in this time and place is very dangerous." Ezat dabbed Pax's face with a damp rag.

Pax closed his eyes and faded in and out of consciousness.

When he next awoke he heard the words, "The spleen is the most likely organ to be damaged during torture of this kind." Pax opened his eyes. The two men talking crouched on either side of him.

"Ezat? Is that you? What is a spleen?" asked Pax. He felt Ezat's hand rest lightly on his arm, but it was the other man who spoke.

"I am Dr. Aria. Point to where it hurts."

He might have laughed. There was no part of his body that was not bleeding, seeping, or bruised. But the pain inside was different. Something inside his body was broken.

Pax rolled onto his side and pointed. Gently, as if his fingers were dancing over hot coals, Dr. Aria touched him. "Turn on your other side," he said, and with Ezat's help, Pax complied.

"It is not the spleen. Your appendix is enlarged," he said simply.

"I don't understand," said Pax.

"The spleen is above the abdomen. It could rupture if hit by a blunt instrument, but the spleen is on the left side. The internal pain you are having is on the right side. It is your appendix."

"What is an appendix?" asked Pax.

"It is an organ. When it is diseased, it is called appendicitis. Roll onto your back, slowly."

Pax did as he was told, although the effort shot spikes of pain up his spine.

The doctor placed his hand on Pax's forehead. "You have a fever."

"Why causes appendic . . . ?" Pax took a breath. It was all confusing.

"It is caused by infection," the doctor said simply.

Again the two men talked about him as Pax turned the doctor's words over in his head. His mind was a muddle. Pax reached up and touched the doctor's sleeve. "Would I have had this appendix even if I was not in here?"

The doctor nodded. "In all likelihood, yes."

"And I would have died on the street."

"I cannot say that for certain," said the doctor. But they all knew, street children we not given expensive operations. Street children had no value.

"And Kai would have been alone," whispered Pax.

The doctor stood and motioned to Ezat. The two men left Pax lying on his cell floor and went out into the hallway. Pax watched. The doctor's feet were bandaged. He was being tortured too.

Ezat returned. "I have clean bandages and some antiseptic for your feet. More medicine is coming."

"Medicine?" Pax tried to form the word.

"It is from the outside, that is all I can tell you. It is important that you do not know too much." Ezat gently lifted Pax's foot and sprinkled it with water. "This will hurt."

"Hurt?" This time Pax did smile, and maybe Ezat did too.

"You have not lost your sense of humor, Pax," said Ezat.

"Why did the doctor hide a writer?" asked Pax. The pain was not so terrible. Ezat was gentle.

"A writer can tell the world about us, about our cause." Ezat lifted Pax's foot.

"Torture—it is too ugly a word. People will turn away."

"Those who torture are also damaged forever. They are filled with poison. Those who learn about us are enriched and grow powerful." Ezat patted Pax's left foot dry, then dribbled the red antiseptic onto Pax's open sores slowly.

"What is a *cause?*" hissed Pax through clenched teeth. The pain was increasing. The medicine Ezat was dabbing on his feet stung like a hundred bees.

"Our cause is simple—the right to vote, freedom to say what we think, freedom to write what we feel. Do you know the expression 'the pen is mightier than the sword'?"

Ezat wrapped one foot in a clean bandage. Pax cringed but shook his head.

"It is from a poem by Edward Bulwer-Lytton. *'Beneath the rule of men entirely great / The pen is mightier than the sword.'*" Ezat tied up the bandage and picked up Pax's right foot. "What can a sword do? It can kill. But a pen . . . now there is a powerful instrument. It conveys the power of imagination." Ezat started the whole process again with Pax's right foot.

"How . . ." Pax gulped with the pain. "How do you know such things?"

"I am a professor in the university, but poetry is my first love."

"Why are you here?"

"I do not think the government liked my poetry." Again Ezat smiled. The best Pax could manage was a grimace.

"Do I call you 'professor'?" Pax tried to smile but his lips would not curl.

"Students would use the term 'doctor,' not 'professor.' But I do not think titles are necessary in this place. It is enough to think of each other as human beings."

"I know poetry. Teacher . . . he said . . ." Pax lost his breath as Ezat poured the antiseptic on his right foot.

"Tell me, Pax, what did your teacher say?" Ezat spoke in a voice full of compassion and concern.

"He said, 'Don't go back to sleep. You must ask for what you really want. Don't go back to sleep.'"

"Ah, Rumi. Shall I tell you another poem?" asked Ezat.

Pax nodded.

"I will tell you the end of it. It says, 'Do not go gentle into that good night. / Rage, rage against the dying of the light.'" Ezat wrapped the second foot. "Mr. Dylan Thomas wrote the poem about his father's death, but I do believe it means that we are meant to fight until our last breath."

Ezat carried on talking as if the two were walking in a park, his voice steady and reassuring.

"Would it surprise you to know that most of the torturers have families? That they believe that what they are doing is right? That they blame us, the tortured, for making them torture us, for turning them into torturers? That most people will torture under the right circumstances?"

"I could not do this to another human being," whispered Pax.

"I believe you. I believe that you are one of the special people who would not hurt another human being."

"Then you would be wrong. I would kill for . . ." Pax's words drifted.

"No, Pax. It is wrong to kill for love, but it is not wrong to fight for love. There is a difference. Sleep now."

"I want to tell you about Kai, about Goddess Girl." Pax wanted to tell him everything. "Tell Kai that I can fly." And he wanted to tell Ezat about a book, *The Seven Natural Wonders of the World*. About Peter Bennett, the man who gave him the book. And he wanted to talk about Bell and the Pink House.

Pax spoke in stops and starts long into the night.

Chapter 30

"Fifty rations for you." The torturer tied Pax to the bed, face down.

When it was over, he lay there, drifting. He fell in and out of a rocky sleep.

"Young King," Goddess Girl called to him.

He tried to answer. His mouth was thick, dry, lips cracked.

"It is time to go," she said gently.

He tried to move, to turn his head. And then the chains around his wrists and ankles fell away. He crawled off the bed. He stood and staggered forward. With each step he grew in strength.

"That's right, come to me." Goddess Girl flapped her giant wings. "Climb on my back, Young King. We will fly." Goddess Girl's laugh was like singing bells.

He threw his leg over her back. He burrowed deep into her feathers. Up they went, high, higher.

He closed his eyes, and when he opened them, there was

Mount Everest, majestic, proud, brutal. He sat up. Energy filled his body, his spirit, and his soul. Goddess Girl spread her wings until they filled the sky. Up she went, soaring between the mountains, then down into crevasses. Below, green trees clung to rocks while craggy, gray stone columns soared up into thin air.

"Hold on." Goddess Girl pulled her wings in close and then swooped between the peaks.

Pax wrapped his arms round her neck and held tight. "I can see!" he cried, and then out came a great laugh that echoed from mountain to mountain. A glistening frost coated his lips and teeth. His hair was as white as the snow, his body warmed by her feathers.

"Where to now?" she cried.

"The Great Barrier Reef!" Pax raised his face to the sun.

"Hold tight."

Goddess Girl turned south. Her wings grew long, longer than a ship's sail, longer than his eyes could see. Longer and longer until they touched the horizon on either side. And then she tucked her giant wings in tight, pointed her head down. The air turned soft and warm. The frost melted away and he stood, his feet planted on Goddess Girl's back.

"Ya-hoo!" he cried.

"Do you see?" she cried, her voice caught on the wind.

"I see, I see!" And again Pax let out a resounding howl. It was the Great Barrier Reef. From high up the water was puckered, while closer to land whitecaps curled like tiny hands. Each wave beckoned to him, welcoming him. *Come, come*, said the waves.

"Hold on tight, Young King."

Goddess Girl plunged into the water. There they were, millions of fish, each one more beautiful than the next. Spotted fish, dotted fish, striped fish, creatures that crawled along the sea floor.

Pax saw something that had wings like a bat but moved with the grace of a bird. "What is that?" he shouted. Wait. He could talk underwater! He could breathe, too!

"It is the great manta ray." Goddess Girl's voice was full of bubbles.

Like a whale breaching the surf, they rose up into the air and flew.

"Where to now?" said Goddess Girl.

"The Grand Canyon," cried Pax.

In the blink of an eye they were there. They glided through the canyon, the soaring red walls on either side creating a cradle. And then Goddess Girl swooped down and perched at the highest point and gazed down into the canyon's great crevasses. For many moments they took in Earth's glory.

"They are mountains that go down!" laughed Pax.

"Agggggh," he cried. The pain in his side was sudden, like a knife carving up his insides.

"Help," he cried. "Help me."

"I am here, Pax." Ezat dabbed his forehead with a cloth.

"Where is here?" Pax spoke in short, labored breaths.

"You are in prison. You are delirious. The doctor has come many times. You were given some drugs for the pain. They will not last. Close your eyes. I will not leave you."

Ezat appeared above Pax like a ghost, his body wavering in the shadows.

"Can you hear me, Pax? Squeeze my hand if you understand me."

Pax felt Ezat's hand in his. He forced his fingers to curl around Ezat's hand.

"The government has made a decision." Ezat paused.

"Yes?" Speech was difficult but he could still think.

"They will execute you tomorrow morning."

Pax felt Ezat's touch.

"Pax, it is me, Dr. Aria. Your appendix is inflamed. It will burst any time." Pax turned his head. The drugs were wearing off. A searing arrow of pain exploded in his head. In a flash everything turned white.

"Can you hear me? If you can, blink twice," said the doctor.

Pax blinked twice. "If your appendix bursts, you will die in great pain, worse pain than you have now. If you live until morning, they will hang you. We have a drug. It will put you to sleep but you will not wake up. You have to tell us what to do. It must be your decision."

Pax could see the faces of both men clearly. He wanted to say thank-you. "How?" The word came out in a puff.

"How, what? How did we get the drugs? Is that what you are asking? They were smuggled in."

"Ezat? Hanging . . . not good for children . . . to see . . ."

"Pax, it is no failure to take destiny into your own hands."

"Yes," Pax whispered. "I will take the drug."

The doctor slipped a needle into a vein in Pax's arm. Pax could feel Ezat leaning over him, his ear resting just above Pax's mouth.

Pax's words were gurgles, little more than sputters. "Kai, find Kai . . . the boy . . . Tell him. Please, find him. Tell him . . . he has his own destiny . . . I have mine." It took everything, everything he had to say those simple words.

He breathed in and out. In. Out. Life in, life out. Which is the last breath? In. Out.

Goddess Girl stood behind the doctor in the far corner of the cell.

"You have done your best. You are brave and true." Her words surrounded him like birdsong.

Goddess Girl grew and grew. She held her wings aloft as if welcoming him home.

"Ezat, see. Look behind you!" Pax gasped.

Ezat followed the direction of Pax's gaze. He took a minute, turned back, and said, "Yes, she is beautiful. The world may never know, but we know, you have fought well, my young friend. You have betrayed no one." Ezat lowered his head and let tears roll down his face.

"Dr. Ezat, don't cry."

"What is this?" Stink Boy filled the doorway. He looked at Pax, Ezat, the doctor, the needle. "What have you done?" Stink Boy screamed as he kicked the empty syringe out of the doctor's hand. There was a great pause.

The curl in Stink Boy's lip softened. He waited, unsure. Ezat looked up into Stink Boy's eyes. Stink Boy's face emptied. He turned away and shuffled down the hall.

"He's a boy," whispered Pax.

"Just a boy . . ." Ezat touched Pax's forehead. "Go now, my young friend. May all that you have learned in this life help you in your continuing journey. Godspeed."

Pax's hand opened and out rolled a tiny bread sculpture. It was the image of Kai.

"Come, Young King," said Goddess Girl.

Pax floated up to the top of the cell and gazed down at Ezat and the doctor. A long, cool breath left him, and with it went pain. He could no longer feel his body, no longer move a leg, or an arm, or a finger. He spoke, but his mouth did not move. He said, "I love you all," but the words were not heard.

"Don't look back. Just come." Her voice was full of song.

Pax climbed on the back of Goddess Girl and in an instant they were soaring up into the clouds. The wind cleaned him and the sun warmed him.

"Where are we going?"

"To Beauty."

"Where is Beauty?" he cried into the wind.

"It is a place fit for a king."

The sea vanished. The earth released its mighty hold. Above the clouds was the sun, above the sun was darkness, above darkness were shafts of brilliant light. And then he saw her. Beauty, in all her glory.

Chapter 31

Ten years later - Oxford University

High above, birds perched on spires, pinnacles, and peaks, and there were thousands to choose from. Oxford, England, was called "the city of dreaming spires" for a reason.

Two young students ran across the green grass of Christ Church, a college of Oxford University, then disappeared through the great wooden doors of an ancient building.

Henry Ainsworth-Smith opened Kai's inside door, burst into Kai's room, and flopped down on the only chair not piled with books and clothes. The outside door to Kai's room, called "the oak," was open, which at Christ Church meant "I am home and receiving."

"Hey, Kai, your mobile is off. The Bulldogs are trying to call you from the gate."

The Bulldogs were neither dogs nor police. And they were no longer officially called Bulldogs. They were now called "Proctors' Officers," defenders of the gate and all things

PRISON BOY • 191

orderly, but given that Oxford University did not change traditions easily, the ancient nickname stuck.

Albert Wang, puffing from the three-story climb, stomped up the stairs behind Henry and leaned against the doorframe.

"In or out. Don't stand there like an empty bottle," said Kai.

Henry shook his head. "You sound like my grandmother."

Albert gazed over at Kai's unmade bed. "You need a *bedder.*"

Kai pulled a face. Bed-makers for students had not been around for years, but Albert lived in another decade . . . or century, maybe.

"Haven't you packed up yet?" Henry put his hands on his hips and looked around. It was end of term. All of Oxford was emptying, only to be refilled shortly by conference attendees who would pay to stay in the vacant rooms. Men and women from all over the world would soon walk the grounds wearing name badges.

"I'm not leaving until next week." Kai stood in his boxer briefs, his hands holding a pair of pants.

Kai had upper-floor rooms in Peckwater Quadrangle, Christ Church. The rooms were paneled in oak with high ceilings. He'd scored a corner room, the best of the best.

Of course he could have lived *out* like Henry and Albert, but he liked living in Peck. Anyway, even though he was finishing his final year, he was the same age as the first-year students who lived there, eighteen. Except for Henry, Albert, and Althea, of course, everyone in his graduating year was twenty-one or older.

"What do they want?" Kai pulled on his pants, then yanked a jumper over his head.

"Who?" asked Henry as he flipped through one of Kai's final essays.

"The Bulldogs."

"There is a man wanting to see you at the gate." Henry tossed the paper aside and ducked into a small alcove off Kai's room. It was a tiny kitchen that held a small fridge, a kettle, and a shelf stacked with energy bars. Henry opened Kai's fridge and pulled out a bottle of something green. He peered at the bottle's label, his mouth pursed, his forehead crumpled.

Kai glanced at Henry and grinned. They had shared a room in their first year. Albert had lived across the hall back then. They had all been admitted to Christ Church, Oxford, when they were fourteen years old. They were gifted, brilliant perhaps. Althea was smarter than all of them put together.

"It's here somewhere." Kai tossed around books and clothes in search of his mobile. He pulled back the covers on his bed, then peered into his garbage bin. He'd just had it! He had already texted Althea today telling her that he could meet for lunch.

Henry twisted the cap off the bottle and sniffed. "It smells like compost." He wrinkled his nose.

"Albert, are you sitting on my mobile?" Kai looked over at Albert, who picked up the paper Henry had tossed aside.

"No." He didn't look up.

Henry took a swig of the juice. "Mother of . . . it's disgusting." His face curled up like a cooked shrimp.

"It's a vitamin drink. It's expensive," said Kai.

"Shades of Mummy doting on her baby boy. What's next? Daddy coming to pack you up? You know the Yanks would call your *mater* a helicopter-mom."

"His mother is more like a drone," mumbled Albert. "You know—*zzzzzzzzz*—watching from afar."

"I thought the whole point of drones was that they were silent. Henry, ring my mobile." Kai tossed the pillows back on his bed.

"It's the only-child thing. Thank God I have three brothers. Did I tell you my little brother just got expelled from Harrow? The parents are so upset they don't know that I'm alive. It's lovely. God bless idiot brothers."

Albert and Kai exchanged knowing looks. Henry himself was nearly sent down from Christ Church after getting mixed up with some much older boys—drinking and carrying on.

"Never mind. Here it is." Kai unearthed his phone from a pile of laundry and peered at the screen. "It's dead. Did you see who it was?"

Kai went to the window and looked out over the quad. From his room, third floor, upper right, he could see Christ Church Library on the south side of the quad. To the southeast was Canterbury Quadrangle, to the southeast Oriel Square and Canterbury Gate.

"Who?" Albert flipped to the end of Kai's final paper on string theory.

"Who what?" said Henry.

"The guy at the gate. Did you get a look at him?" Kai plugged in his phone.

"I don't know. He looked foreign," said Henry.

Albert waved Kai's paper around. "I get the part about string theory being a hypothetical outline in which the point-like particles of particle physics are replaced by one-dimensional objects called strings, but—"

"Then you're doing pretty well for a philosophy student. You'll notice I don't mention Kierkegaard even once. But it's not hypothetical, it's theoretical. Just skip to the conclusion," said Kai. "And what do you mean by 'He looked foreign'?" Kai asked Henry.

Albert's parents were Chinese but he'd grown up in London, in a neighborhood called Golders Green. Henry was born in Northern Ireland, moved to India, grew up in Russia, spent two years in Indonesia, and then three years in Texas, which, according to Henry, was not really part of America but a country in its own right.

"What does *foreign* look like?" said Kai.

"He means artsy," Albert said. "Next week we will practice political correctness in Western society." Albert rolled up Kai's paper and used it to bat a fly.

Henry left the energy drink on the desk and went back into Kai's fridge.

"Albert, pass me your mobile," said Kai.

Albert whipped it at his head. Kai snapped it out of the air like a salamander catching a fly. Kai was a wicket keeper for his college cricket squad.

Kai punched in the code for the front gate and announced himself. "Is there a guest there for me? . . . Who? . . . Dr. Ampior from Cairo University? He must have the wrong person. Can you make sure he wants to meet me?"

Kai looked out the window. He could see students, dons, and professors walking to and from classes, a few in gowns, several on bicycles.

"Kai, what's wrong? You look very vampire-ish, deathly white," said Albert, in a ghoulish tone.

Kai brushed him away. "Yes. Tell him that I will meet him downstairs. Thank you." Kai hung up.

"Who is he?" asked Henry.

"Just . . . someone who knows . . . my father." Kai was not a good liar at the best of times. "Out, I have to tidy." He tossed the mobile back to Albert and pushed the two out of the room.

"I thought we were going out." Henry popped open a can of ice tea.

"I'll catch up with you later." Kai slammed the doors.

"We love you too," cried Henry from the hallway.

Kai moved around the room at lightning speed. Whoever he was, *he knew Pax.* Cairo University, Egypt—that part didn't make sense. How would Pax know someone from Egypt? Maybe it was a friend of Bell's . . . ? There was no reason to be nervous, but his heart was thumping all the same.

Kai tossed last night's pizza crust in the bin and kicked his laundry under the bed. The cricket bat and bag were stuffed into the closet. He snapped shut his laptop. His desk was covered in papers, and there was something else, the photograph taken on the porch at the Pink House with Bell, Pax—all of them. He opened the top drawer and, with one long sweep of his arm, tried to push as much mess as possible, computer too, into the drawer. The photograph did not fit.

196 • SHARON E. McKAY

He looked around for a spot to hide it and then noticed white boxers on the bedpost. He dropped the photo and stuffed the underwear under his pillow, then took another look out the window.

There were dozens of people milling around the quad and yet Kai spotted him right off, walking on the curvy paths towards Peck. He was tall, thin, and walked with a halting gate. He used a walking stick. It was hard to tell what he looked like from a distance but he did not look *artsy* exactly. More like *exotic*.

Kai glanced around his room. A disaster. Maybe they would go for a coffee.

He bolted out the door, but even as his feet thumped down the steps, his thoughts, memories, overwhelmed him. It was hard to breathe. He stopped on the stairs, leaned against the wall, and rubbed his face with the back of his hand. He was sweating. He tried not to think about Pax, Bell, Mega, or any of them. He pushed his thoughts into a box and slammed the lid shut—like the door in the prison. It was a forever sound, a final sound.

It was if he had been born on the day the wheels of the plane touched down at Heathrow Airport outside London. Peter had sat on one side of him and Nadia on the other. His new life had begun that day. Parents. Home. School.

What did this man want?

Kai took one deep breath, then another, before continuing down the stairs. He swung open Peck's great wooden doors. He held out his hand to the tall, thin man in front of him.

"I'm Kai."

"How do you do. My name is Dr. Ezat Ampior. You are, I believe, the friend of Pax's."

Kai nodded.

"You were a hard young man to find." Ezat Ampior looped the crook of his cane over his arm and extended his hand.

Chapter 32

"How *did* you find me?" asked Kai. They stood facing each other in the doorway.

The man, Dr. Ezat Ampior, was white-haired, sharp-featured, gaunt yet stately, like a military man, except crooked—he favored the right side of his body. But, for all his presence, he was as delicate as bird.

"I came upon a journal that mentioned you as one of the up-and-coming talents of the physics world. Your name, Kai, is unusual, but also your last name, Bennett, caught my attention. I had heard of a Peter Bennett. He is a man I admire, a man of great courage. Among other things, he had medicine smuggled into the prison . . . but I am getting ahead of myself."

A thousand questions were tumbling around Kai's head. Where to start? He was vaguely aware that he was breathing hard.

"Where are you from?"

"I teach at Cairo University."

"Are you a professor?" asked Kai.

"Poetry, English, Arabic studies," said Dr. Ampior. "Perhaps we could sit? Standing for any length of time is troublesome. A park bench, perhaps?"

The doctor's voice was quiet, more of a hum. There was a depth to his eyes that was both mesmerizing and sad. What would make a man look like that? But the question Kai had yet to ask out loud was, *Why are you here?*

"We could go out for coffee, or I could make you tea or coffee in my rooms. It's instant, I'm afraid. I'm on the third floor." Kai was sure this frail man would not want to climb three sets of stairs.

"If you don't mind climbing slowly, I would welcome a cup of tea."

Dr. Ampior climbed the stairs like a child. One hand clutched the rail, the other his cane. He took a step, rested both feet on the same step, and then took another step. Kai could hear the man's breathing—slow, labored, like someone who was a heavy smoker or suffered from lung disease. It took an age to reach the third floor.

Kai's name, Kai Bennett, written in white lettering, was above the doorframe. Kai swung open the first door, "the oak," and then the inside door. His heart was pounding.

"May I?" The doctor pointed to a chair between Kai's desk and bookshelf.

"Yes, please." Kai lurched ahead to clear off the chair.

"Perhaps a glass of water?" asked the doctor. Kai rinsed a glass in the alcove sink, poured some water in it, and plugged in the kettle.

The doctor sipped the water slowly, his Adam's apple bobbing with every swallow.

"Why were you looking for me?" Finally, the question came out.

The doctor put the glass on Kai's desk, reached into his pocket, and pulled out a handkerchief. Kai thought he would use it to dab his forehead but instead he peeled back the folds as though he were peeling a banana.

"I made a promise to a brave young man. He asked me to find you. I believe he would have wanted you to have this." He held out his hand.

Kai peered at a strange little object in the doctor's palm. It was a sculpture of a child.

"It is made of bread," the doctor continued. "I took the liberty some years ago of having it preserved. I had it done professionally, by an art restorer. I was afraid that it might fall apart before I found you." He placed the sculpture in Kai's hand.

Kai's breath caught in his throat. It was as if he had been walking on ice only to slip and plunge into deep, bitterly cold water. He sat down on the edge of his bed. Ezat stood above him, although Kai did not remember him getting up out of the chair and crossing the room.

The object had no real color and the form was crude. Still, Kai could see what others could not—brown shorts and yellow shirt, matted hair, bony legs with knobby knees.

"Pax?" Kai whispered.

"He made it in prison. Perhaps I could get *you* a glass of water?" Ezat spoke gently.

"No, please. I will make tea." He wanted out, to run away, if only for a few minutes. Kai placed the little figure on the bookshelf, stood back to make sure it would not tip over, then went off to make tea.

He stood above the kettle and waited for it to boil. His hands shook. His knees threatened to give out. He hung his head, then leaned back against the wall and closed his eyes.

When the kettle whistled he made the tea, prepared a plate, and took a deep breath.

"Biscuits?" Kai held out a plate of Nadia's homemade cookies.

The doctor was standing in front of Kai's bookshelf. "Thank you." He did not turn around.

"Professor Ampior, do you take milk in your tea? It is just Tetley's, I'm afraid. And I don't have lemon." Kai held up a small glass that doubled as a creamer.

"Please, call me Ezat. We do not use the title *professor* for people with Ph.D. degrees. We use Dr. as a prefix or Ph.D. at the end of the name. I personally prefer my name without any title. No milk, thank you." As Ezat accepted the tea, Kai noticed the man's scarred hands.

Ezat sipped the tea, then reached for a book by Rumi. "You like poetry." Was it a question or a statement? Kai nodded. Ezat turned to place the cup on the edge of the desk. The photograph on Kai's desk caught his eye. "And this?" Ezat picked the picture up.

Kai cringed. He had forgotten about it. "I, we, Pax and I . . . lived in an orphanage. It was called the Pink House. It was painted pink. Peter, my father, took the picture. Nadia, my mother, had it framed. I didn't mean to bring it with me . . . to college . . . but she slipped it into my bag . . ." Kai's voice trailed off.

Ezat nodded. "And who are they?" he asked.

Kai had no choice but to stand behind him and point.

"That is Santoso, Bambang. I am in front. That's Bell, who ran the orphanage. She died many years ago. That's Mega, Bhima, and Guntur at the end." He skipped over Pax.

"Do you keep in touch with them?" Ezat asked.

Kai shook his head. "My mother, Nadia, talks to Bell's sister in London. She is in touch with them." There was a note of regret in his voice, or perhaps embarrassment.

"Do you know where they are now?" asked Ezat.

"Mega is a nurse. She is married with two children. Bambang drives a train. He has two children, too. Bhima is in university."

"It is wonderful that they have all done well, but their education must be expensive!" said the professor.

"Bell's sister pays for their education," said Kai.

"And these two?" He pointed to Guntur and Santoso.

"They were in an accident when they were kids. The Red Cross arranged medical care for them. They were adopted after that. I think Guntur is an apprentice to an electrician, and Santoso is a chef," said Kai.

The professor nodded and pointed to Pax. "Pax was a handsome young man."

Kai twitched. He took the photograph and slipped it back in the drawer. "Where did you meet him?" Kai asked the question simply, with a breezy air. Of course he knew the answer. Prison.

Ezat began. He spoke without drama, without inflection. Great Tom, the bell in the clock tower, struck noon. An hour had passed. Kai's shoulders sagged despite his best efforts to sit up straight.

"Perhaps you are aware that we were tortured," said Ezat.

Kai nodded. Perhaps he did know, as one knows things in the bones. But did he know it in his heart and mind? No.

Ezat went on. Another hour passed. Pax was beaten. He withered away in pain day and night for weeks. He was constantly thirsty. Hunger did to his body inside what the torture did to it outside. There was a wall—women and children were imprisoned behind it. There was a jailer named Stink Boy and a giant bird Pax called a goddess. She had wings, a crown of jewels, and blue eyes that sparkled like sapphires. Pax flew on her back. There were soldier birds with gold beaks.

Through it all Kai's face remained composed, his body still, rigid. In his mind, he was raging. He was at the bottom of a well screaming up into the light.

"Pax found comfort in his imagination. He loved poetry. He loved stories. He loved you. Towards the end he was obsessed with the Seven Natural Wonders of the World. He said that he had seen them, flown over them. He could describe them in amazing detail."

"Yes, as children we had a book. Here." Kai's voice, even to his ears, was surprisingly controlled. He pulled the book from his bookshelf. "It is not the same book, of course. We were given the original when we lived in the orphanage. I found this one a few years ago in Arcadia, a secondhand bookshop off St. Michael's Street." Kai handed Ezat the book. Why did he say that? What did it matter where the book came from? He was sweating.

"Ah, this is why Pax could describe the places so accurately." Nodding, Ezat flipped through the pages. He did not seem surprised. He paused as if considering, perhaps struggling, with what to say next. "He was delirious towards the end. He was infatuated with this Goddess Girl. She gave him peace, perhaps resolution."

"There was a poster on a wall when we lived with Ol' May, the woman who took us in after the orphanage was closed. Pax loved that poster. So did I." Containing his emotions was getting harder.

"That explains it," Ezat said softly. He placed the book on the shelf and sat back down in the chair.

To Kai's eyes Ezat looked calm—too calm. Rage rushed up Kai's throat. His legs felt like jelly. The other part of his brain—the part that analyzed, observed, kept him sane— thought, *Why did he come here? What does he want? And why is he trying to turn Pax's death into some sort of fantasy?* Then there was the other part of his brain—the part that felt wounded. He thought, *This is what it feels like to have a soul ripped away from a spirit.*

Kai rocked back and forth on his heels. He thought he might be sick, and then words rushed out.

"Pax did not visit the Seven Natural Wonders of the

World. He did not fly on the back of a great winged, diamond-studded bird. It is all nonsense." He spoke through clenched teeth. "Pax was a teenager. He died at the hands of monsters, and here you are telling me a story about winged creatures? Trying to say that the imagination is a way to fight torture is like telling a man to hold back the ocean with his hands." Kai stopped, breathless. His face was red, his ears hot. For a moment they were both surrounded by a thick, suffocating silence.

"I apologize. I have hurt you. Pax died in my arms. I had hoped . . ." The old man bobbed his head slowly. The sadness in his eyes intensified. Cane in hand, he stood and slowly shuffled towards the door. "I must go. Perhaps, another time . . ."

Kai did not look up. He heard the two doors close and muffled footsteps on the stairs.

He waited. He opened the doors and listened. He counted each step. The old man was on the second-floor landing. More steps—he was in the downstairs hall. Door opened. Closed. Gone.

Kai closed both his doors—tight. He roared like an injured animal. He raised his fists in the air and pounded his mattress. He lifted it up over his head and threw it against the wall. He knocked over the tea tray, smashed whatever he could reach. He did it over and over again. With his hands cupping his face, he cried.

Exhausted, Kai slid down onto his haunches and pressed his forehead against the wall. He could smell lemon wax that had been polished into the centuries-old wood.

He hung his head. His chin bobbed on his chest. If his head fell off its stem and rolled on the floor, he would be dead. The pain would stop. He would be at peace.

Kai staggered to his feet, went to the window, and looked out onto the quad. Everything remained as it had been two hours ago, a year ago, hundreds of years ago. But now he could also see Pax tied to a bed and beaten until bloody. Fifty lashes a day. *Rations* they called it.

Kai grabbed hold of the windowsill and then turned. There it was—the tiny sculpture. He picked it up in his hands and cradled it against his chest. Pax must have been hungry. He must have wanted to eat the bread. Instead he had made this for him, a gift.

"I should not have left you there. Pax, I'm sorry." Kai lifted his face to the ceiling and howled like a dog at the moon, except there was no moon and he wasn't a dog—he was just a boy, alone, and forgiveness was nowhere in sight.

Why? Why torture a boy? Why torture anyone? The questions pulsed in his head. *Why do people do this to each other? Animals don't torture each other. Just people. WHY?*

"*Why? Why do all children ask 'why'?*" said Bell. Her voice was back. He had locked all the voices away, and now they were back.

Kai looked down at the tiny sculpture. "Pax, did you really believe that this would be given to me? The odds . . ." And, like all revelations, it came suddenly, without warning. And then there was clarity. Kai knew. HE KNEW!

Kai's eyes darted around the room. It was a mess. Wallet. Where? There. Mobile? He flung clothes aside and reached under a pile of papers that had fallen on the floor. There. He unplugged his mobile, ran down the stairs, out the door, and sprinted across the quad.

"Hey, Kai, wait up." Albert jogged towards him. "Where are you going? Althea said that you two were going out to lunch. Henry and I . . . What's wrong with you? Slow down."

"Tell Althea that I will call her, okay? Just tell her that." Kai kept on running. His heart beat hard, his arms pumped.

Two Bulldogs stood at the gate.

"Good morning, sir." A Bulldog tipped his hat.

Kai nodded back and gulped air. "There was a man here, Dr. Ampior from Cairo University. He was using a cane. Which way did he go?"

"He took a cab, sir. I heard him tell the driver to take him to the train station."

Kai stepped out on the road. Luck. An empty taxi.

Chapter 33

Kai barged through the train station. It was not yet midday. Summer tourists had replaced students and commuters. An American, by the sound of her voice, spoke to a legless man in a wheelchair, then dropped a few coins into his cup.

"*An American tourist is coming to give us money,*" said Pax. The voice came out of the fog. More words that he had locked away were filtering back.

Kai spun around, once, twice. "Have I missed the train to London?" he asked a ticket-taker.

"I'd say. But there will be another along in an hour, every hour on the hour," replied the man.

He had missed Ezat, likely by just minutes.

Kai sat down on a bench. He rubbed his hands across his face, up into his hair, and down the back of his neck. He could find him again, of course. Cairo University. But now, he wanted to talk to the man *now, now, now.* Kai closed his eyes.

"Please, please tell me." Kai hugged his knees into his chest, and leaned his head against Pax's shoulder.

Pax took a deep breath. *"On a planet far away, past all the stars and heaven too, a beautiful queen had a baby. War came to the planet. The queen asked a magician to save her baby from the enemy. The magician used his wand to create a rainbow. The queen put the baby on the rainbow and the baby slid down to earth."*

"Kai?"

Kai looked up into Ezat's face. Ezat stood above him, shoulders hunched, head forward as if walking against a wind.

"I thought that I had missed..." Kai leapt up and stammered out the words.

"I did miss the train. I wish I had even a bit of the strength of my youth." He smiled sadly.

"I came ... I came to apologize."

"There is nothing to apologize for. I should not have told you as much as I did, certainly not in one conversation." He looked tired.

"Could you stay a little while longer? There's a train every hour."

"I must sit." Ezat sat down on a bench, both hands cupping the knob of his cane. Kai sat beside him.

"Was it hard on you—your time in prison?" What a stupid question. He could have kicked himself.

"It was harder on my wife and infant son." Ezat spoke sadly, without anger.

Strands of the story came back to Kai—the wall, women and children behind the wall. Were his wife and son behind the wall?

"How, I mean, why were you arrested?" Kai stopped. Perhaps that was too personal a question. Nothing he said seemed right.

"They called me a radical. I was a poet, a professor. The police came in the middle of the night. My wife was feeding our baby. She did not even have time to reach for the diaper bag." Ezat took a deep breath. "But I think you have heard enough sad stories today."

"Is that why you took such good care of Pax, because you could not care for your own son?" Kai asked.

"All the political prisoners cared for the children. We gave them the best food and tried to find them medicine. In a place where we were treated worse than animals, I found some comfort in caring for him," said Ezat.

The tears in Kai's eyes were sudden. Anything left of anger in Kai had evaporated.

"How did you get out of prison?" he asked, gently.

"Several months after Pax died, I was told to go home, and so I did. There was no reason, no explanation, just an open door. Only then did I learn that my wife and son had died months after our arrest. Perhaps it is best that I did not know. I would have given up."

"Have you . . . did you . . . I mean, are you over it?"

Ezat thought for a moment. "I sleep with the lights on, like a small boy. In the dark, when I close my eyes, I hear screams. No more . . ." Ezat stood and stumbled. Kai grabbed his elbow. "I'm sorry. I did not mean . . . Could you stay? Maybe just for lunch?" Kai was suddenly desperate. "Please, I need to know . . ." His voice drifted.

Ezat paused. He nodded and then, as if changing channels on a television, he said, brightly, "Perhaps I could treat you to a bit of what you Brits call pub fare. And maybe you could tell me how it is that a boy such as yourself ended up at Oxford." Ezat smiled.

Chapter 34

"This way." The hostess showed them to a dark, woody booth with deep leather seats. It was late spring, but still a small fire burned in an open hearth. "Your server will take your order."

For a moment the two perused the menu.

"Decided?" asked Ezat. Kai nodded. They closed their menus.

Ezat waited, patiently.

Kai considered. He never spoke about the past—ever. His mother and father often tried to get him to talk, to open up. He refused. "When you are ready . . . ," Nadia, his mother, would say. Then she would add, "We love you."

He sometimes thought that his mum and dad were the gentlest people on earth, and he was the luckiest. Not because he'd won a strange sort of life-lottery, but because he had been loved every minute of his life. First by Pax, and then by Bell, and now by Nadia and Peter . . . and maybe Althea, too.

"You do not talk about your past," said Ezat.

Kai shook his head. "There was a door . . . in the prison. It was made of metal. It slammed shut. I was on one side of the door and Pax was on the other. I never saw him again." Kai held himself very still.

"And I have forced you to open the door," said Ezat quietly.

"Yes."

"My name is Tamarah. I am your server today. Ready to order?" Tamarah hovered above them both. She had a wave of pink in her hair. The tattoo that trailed up her arm said "*Carpe Diem.*"

Kai looked at the closed menu as if he had never seen it before in his life.

"Soup of the day," said Ezat, and to Kai he added, "A lasting effect of my time in prison is a delicate stomach."

Prison? Tamarah's eyes widened.

"I'll have the same," said Kai. He didn't ask what kind of soup. He didn't care. Nor, apparently, did Ezat.

"Anything to drink?" Her eyes went from one to the other.

"Water, please, and tea," said Ezat.

"The same," said Kai. But he didn't want tea any more than he wanted soup.

Tamarah picked up the menus and went on her way.

"Please, go on," said Ezat.

Kai hesitated and began again. "I didn't know what was happening. I suppose I was screaming for Pax. I walked into a bright room. A man stood in front of a barred window. He turned. It was Peter, Dr. Peter Bennett. I had met him before,

214 • SHARON E. MCKAY

you see. He had been kind to me. He opened his arms and I fell into them."

Tamarah set the table with utensils wrapped in napkins, paper placemats, and glasses of water. She placed a basket of buns and a plate of butter in front of them.

"There was a white truck outside. No guards, no guns. The sunlight was shocking. He held me tight. I was seven years old but small for my age and weak from hunger. I could hear gravel crunching under his feet, a car door opening, and a woman's voice. She said, 'Put him beside me.' He tucked me into the backseat of the vehicle. She smelled sweet, like flowers. Her first words were, 'My name is Nadia. I am Peter's wife. You are safe now.' I felt a strap circle my middle and then a click. She said that the seatbelt would keep me safe."

"But how . . . I don't mean to pry . . ." Ezat's voice trailed off.

"How did he know that we were in prison?" said Kai.

Ezat nodded.

"The photograph, the one taken by the security camera, went around the world. Today they would say it went *viral*. Peter saw the picture in an English newspaper. He recognized us.

"The words above the picture said 'Terrorists held in custody.' Below the picture it said, 'Street Boys Become Boy Terrorists.' I didn't even know what a terrorist was. Peter said that the government wanted to clean up the streets. Now they had an excuse to round up the street children.

"Peter still had contacts in the government. He convinced

someone, somewhere, that executing a seven-year-old would make the government look bad. Worse, it would make the government's allies pull their support. Britain, America, and most of Western Europe supported the King and his regime at the time."

Tamarah brought the soup. She placed the bowls on the paper placemats.

"We lived in a hotel for weeks. Peter went away every morning and returned every night. I was desperately worried about Pax, but I fully expected Peter to walk through the door with him. I believed that adults could do anything.

"One afternoon Peter came bursting into the hotel shouting, 'We must go, now!' Nadia told me to put on my shoes and new jacket. I didn't know how to do lace-ups. I just stood on the spot and watched Nadia and Peter run in circles. I knew something that they did not. I was not going anywhere without Pax.

"There were travel documents on the table. One had a great seal on the bottom, fancy letters at the top, and many signatures. And there was my name—Kai Bennett, son of Nadia Bennett, Ph.D., and Peter Bennett, Ph.D., of Oxford, England. I should have leapt around the room with joy—I should have been happy, at the very least. For the first time in my life I had parents. Instead I screamed, 'PAX!'

"That's when Peter told me that Pax had died of a burst appendix. Nadia slipped the new jacket over my arms. She put shoes by my feet and magically my feet slipped into them." Kai sipped water.

"Would you like some dessert?" asked Tamarah. The two shook their heads and waited silently as she cleared the table.

Kai stopped. He had lost the thread.

"You were talking about leaving the hotel."

Kai nodded. "We drove through the city. I could see the area that was bombed. I think I may have cried out. Peter told the driver to go around it."

"Yes. Peter told the driver to go around it. The car lurched in stops and starts and changed lanes many times. We came to a large road. And there it was—the village, my home. The car stopped to let a truck squeeze in ahead. I put one hand on the button of my seatbelt and the other on the door handle. I leapt out of the car and ran out into traffic.

"Nadia was screaming. I just kept running. Cars flew around me. There were honks and shouts. I knew the streets. I knew how to dodge traffic. I kept running. In that moment I really believed that Pax would be around the next corner. Everything would go back to what it was.

"But there was nothing, just a large, open space. Bulldozers were parked ahead on a small hill. Everything was gone. The huts, the sheds, the laneways, the people . . . Where did the people go?

"Peter and Nadia found me wandering about, dragging my feet, I guess. I suppose I was in shock. Nadia put her arms around me. 'You are not alone. You will never be alone again. I promise you.' She was whispering, but I wasn't listening. I had had enough of promises.

"We came to England. Weeks, months went by, and then

I began to create another life. It was easier, you see, to start again. It was easier to just *not remember.*"

"But living here must have been hard, all the same?" said Ezat with a pained smile.

Kai smiled back. "Learning how to deal with *abundance* was a challenge."

"Yes, yes." Ezat nodded. "I had a full life before entering prison—a home, family, a car. But after prison I do recall stepping into a shop and seeing all the fruits and vegetables, row after row of tinned goods, prepared foods—the meats behind glass—it made me dizzy."

Kai grimaced and nodded. He felt his shoulders relax.

"And you adjusted," said Ezat.

Kai nodded. "I guess I had been in England a year when we passed a bakery and I saw a donut in a window. I said, 'That's like me—empty in the middle.' Nadia stood there, right on the sidewalk, and put her head in her hands. I said, 'Mum, I'm sorry. Don't cry.' That was the first time I called Nadia mum. It made her cry all over again." This time Kai smiled. "She has been mum ever since."

There was a pause, but not an uncomfortable one, as Kai tried to regroup and remember where he had left off.

"Soon after, I discovered football. Playing sports made it easy to fit in. And then I discovered physics. I loved mathematics, but physics explained the world. It was calming. I went to Eton. I was home on long leave when the acceptance letter came from Christ Church. I took the letter out into the woods behind our house. I held the paper up to the sky and cried, 'Look, Pax. I have been accepted into Oxford.' I was fourteen years old."

"And, if I may be so bold, how old are you now?"

"Eighteen." Kai grinned. "Except I don't really know the date of my birth. We celebrate my birthday on the day that I landed in England."

Kai's mobile rang. The sound startled them both. Kai looked at the screen.

"It's Althea. I was supposed to meet her for lunch." Kai scowled.

"Then an apology is in order." Ezat signaled for the bill.

Kai's fingers flew over the letters and waited. Her reply was almost instant. "She's going to meet us at the train station."

"Althea would be your girlfriend," said Ezat. This time his smile was bigger, wider.

"I guess, but we've been friends for four years. She's going on to study astrophysics. She has a thing for the stars," said Kai.

It was 3:45 when Kai and Ezat walked slowly down the road towards the train station.

"You seemed uncomfortable when I asked you about the photograph of Bell and the children in the orphanage," said Ezat.

"I was . . ." he said, feeling small, almost petty. He wasn't ashamed of them, he just . . .

"You feel responsible," said Ezat. It was a statement, not a question.

Kai shuddered. His body convulsed. "I should have died with him," he whispered.

"Then you have not listened closely. Pax ultimately died

of a burst appendix. True, it may have been brought on by torture, but perhaps he would have died of it anyway. And then what would have happened to a boy such as yourself on the streets?"

"Are you saying that all of this was some elaborate plan to fulfill my destiny?" Kai was shocked. Surely such an educated man could not have such beliefs?

"There are more things in heaven and earth, Horatio, Than are dreamt of in your philosophy." Ezat smiled. "Shakespeare's *Hamlet*," said Kai. Ezat nodded.

They walked on, slowly and in silence. They could hear the train whistle, like the cry of a bird, distant and unearthly. They walked across the tiled floor and out onto the platform. Again they heard the whistle, nearer now. All faces pointed in the direction of the oncoming train.

"Why do governments torture their enemies *and* their own citizens?" asked Kai. It was too big a question, too complicated to ask now, but he asked it anyway.

"Torture has a long and involved history. I will say this: torture is used by governments and regimes when they become afraid of losing power, when they have lost their moral compass." Ezat spoke quietly. The train lurched into the station and its doors opened.

"Then torture is used by the weak," said Kai.

"Yes," said Dr. Ezat Ampior as he extended his hand.

Kai took it carefully. Would a simple handshake cause him pain?

"I would like to help," said Kai. "I mean, I would like to do something to stop it, if it can be stopped."

"There is an organization to which I belong. I will send you literature."

"Yes. I want to do something. I need to . . . help stop this."

"Tell me, why did you come after me?" asked Ezat.

"I realized that Pax did not send the sculpture as a gift. He sent you. You are the gift." Kai felt the tears in his eyes, in his throat.

"Pax thought perhaps I might be of help to you," said Ezat simply and plainly.

Kai nodded.

Ezat took a step up onto the train, then turned back. "I believe that Pax wanted you to know the whole story. He wanted you to know that in the end he found peace. It is my belief that he wanted you to find peace, too." Ezat boarded the train and sat beside an open window.

"Perhaps I could come to Cairo and visit you." Kai spoke through the train's window.

"I would like that. Bring your parents. They are travelers after all." Ezat smiled.

"You should know that my mum might reorganize your cupboards and change your diet. She's a health-freak," Kai said.

Ezat began to laugh. "I welcome change."

A flock of birds flew overhead. Kai looked up. The birds were tiny specks, flying high above the city of dreaming spires.

"Kai!"

Althea ran towards him down the platform. She wore a green beret, a kilt, and pink stockings. Long, curly red hair fell across her shoulders.

"Dr.—I mean Ezat, this is Althea." Kai smiled broadly. The train lurched forward and began its slow crawl out of the station.

"Hello!" Althea held out her hand. Ezat reached through the window. Their fingertips touched.

Ezat looked into her eyes and saw a shimmering, sparkling cobalt blue that radiated kindness.

"Your eyes . . . such a blue!" Ezat stammered.

"They are not blue!" Kai's laughter rang out as the two ran alongside the slowly moving train.

Ezat put his head out the window. He looked again. Brown eyes—deep, chocolate brown, warm and caring. "Forgive me . . . it must have been the light . . ."

"Good-bye. We'll see you soon," yelled Kai.

"Good-bye," Althea chimed in.

Ezat Ampior sat back in his seat. "Pax," he whispered. "All is as you had hoped."

Author's Note

Thirty years after the United Nations Convention Against Torture called for measures to eliminate torture, the practice still occurs in one hundred and forty-one countries, according to a 2014 report by Amnesty International.

Torture takes root in the shadows but flourishes in the dark. We must bring it out into the open and shine a great light on it. Don't look away. We have the power to stop this. If you would like to join the fight, begin your journey at amnesty.org.

Acknowledgments

The best part of publishing is having a place to thank the people who supported me in many different ways. This book has had a journey all its own, and a long one at that. Patience was needed and freely given.

Canada Council for the Arts and Access Copyright Foundation Research Grant, for their financial support and flexibility. My sincere thanks.

Amnesty International, Alex Neve, Secretary General, Amnesty International, Canada, www.amnesty.ca.

Ezat Mossallanejad, Canadian Centre for Victims of Torture, Toronto, and author of *Religions and the Cruel Return of Gods* (Zagros Editions, 2012). Ezat, the proud father of two and now a widower, was a victim of torture. He is a beautiful man who shared his story freely. While Dr. Ezat Ampior is a creation of the imagination, the torture sequences within these pages are very real and continue today.

Gail Advent Latouche, past deputy director of Corrections Canada, Kandahar, Afghanistan.

Paul D. Milne and Catherine (Cathy) A. Olsiak, who held the wolves at bay, giving me space and time to work.

Editors: Barbara Berson and Catherine Marjoribanks.

Annick Press: Katie Hearn, Patricia Ocampo, Kong Njo, Catherine Dorton, and the staff at Annick Press.

Rob Paterson, a student of History and Human Health, graduate of Christ Church, Oxford.

Barbara Kissick, reader.

David Macleod.

The poem on page 72 is from Mevlâna Jalâluddîn Rumi. Translated by Coleman Barks. http://sufism.org/lineage/rumi/rumi-excerpts/poems-of-rumi-tr-by-coleman-barks-published-by-threshold-books-2